THIS IS YOUR LIFE

JENNIFER ANN SHORE

Print ISBN: 978-1-7360672-4-6

For Steph,
just remember
to breathe

ONE

You can't trust a person who doesn't have any vices.

At least, that's what my dad told me when trying to justify his harmless—his description, not mine—gambling at the penny slots. He spent too many late nights and weekends downtown inside the newly constructed casino while my mom carted my sister and me around to soccer practice (hers), dance rehearsal (again, hers), and art class (yes, still hers).

I've always been more of the bystander type, content to observe and appreciate the world around me, and it's never been more true than recently.

I can simultaneously admire and be confused by the human condition, like how I'm still to this day frustrated by my father's willingness to lose our spare change while understanding the allure of the opportunity to win big.

Thankfully, my own personal vice is harmless.

Well, kind of.

It's not like I'm damaging my liver with bouts of binge

drinking or racking up even more debt on my credit card, but I am indulging in enough calories to count for two meals at once.

My not-so-dirty little non-secret is between me, my metabolism, and a man from Yonkers named Carl who owns my favorite bagel shop.

I'm en route to said establishment, but as much as my mouth is watering in anticipation, I'm not exactly rushing toward my carbohydrate haven.

Instead, I enjoy the walk.

I don't take for granted the fact that I now live in Manhattan. In fact, I appreciate how every single block is like a microcosm of its own, with restaurants, apartments, and every single type of shop someone could ever need.

I definitely miss my family sometimes, but the trade-off of getting to live in Manhattan and experience everything New York has to offer outweighs any desire I have to be in Columbus, Ohio, by at least one million tons.

Since moving almost four months ago, my schedule has been overloaded: chores around the apartment, taking Will to school and his various extracurriculars, and running errands for the Finch family.

I can't complain, though.

Living here always seemed like a far-fetched dream, and I've made it, even though nannying for a wealthy family in the Upper East Side wasn't exactly the reality I imagined for myself.

Still, for the first time in my life, I'm actually making decent money, and although I've only gotten a few direct deposits into my account, the exhilaration of watching the balance on my student loans drop has been worth every single second of being bossed around by Peter and Amanda Finch.

Per their orders, I've successfully delivered Will to school, just like I do every other weekday morning, so I backtrack toward the apartment building.

I'm happy that, by now, I have my bearings enough to know that this is the fastest way to the bagel shop, then to my favorite park by the East River, where I stuff said bagel in my face while I people-watch, then know exactly what streets I need to cross to get on the Q train.

My phone buzzes with a new text message, and I step under the overhang of the Finches' apartment building.

I'm usually a pretty good multitasker, but last week, I tried texting while navigating through Midtown during lunch and got yelled at by at least three people to watch where I was walking. I'm still reeling from it.

It's Bagel Friday, baby!

That's what my sister, Angela, calls my weekly routine.

It's one of the few windows in the week when I have a free block of time, and I take full advantage of it—while also deciding that crumbs and calories do not matter for this occasion.

She fires off a few emojis in celebration, making me smile at her excitement.

She's just as invested in what I'm discovering in New York as I am, insisting I inundate her with photos so she can live vicariously through me while she's finishing up her last year of graphic design school and living at home with our parents.

I send her a selfie from outside the building, then a few

photos as I resume my walk, building up anticipation for both of us at what I'm about to partake in.

At the thought of sinking my teeth into a soft, warm New York bagel slathered in an obscene amount of fluffy cream cheese, my growling stomach signals my feet to move just a little faster.

The door to the tiny shop is propped open, letting in the cooling September air, which mixes with the aroma of freshly baked bread.

"Julianna," Carl says evenly.

"Happy Friday, Carl!" I exclaim.

I don't shy away from my excitement, rubbing my hands together. I avoid the narrowed eyes and pointed looks of the other customers, who are waiting on their coffees and breakfast sandwiches.

It's still early, and judging by the suits and various business attire of my fellow patrons, this is their last moment of peace. After this, they'll be off to fight for space on the subway and spend eight-plus hours in an office downtown, so I can understand them being in their own little worlds.

In fact, New Yorkers have a reputation of being standoffish and rude, but in my experience, it just seems like there are too many people with too much going on for them to indulge in everyday pleasantries and greetings.

The first week here, my cheeks hurt from smiling at everyone I passed on the sidewalk. Most people didn't even meet my gaze, and those who did eyed me like I was about to pull out a knife and stab them.

Since then, I've tried to tone down the Midwestern nice, but given that I barely have any social interaction aside from my two employers and the thirteen-year-old who is too old to even have a nanny, I take what I can get.

"How's Mary today?" I ask Carl.

His very pregnant wife is sweet and talkative, the exact opposite of him.

"Fine."

Before her ankles got too swollen, she helped him in the shop. We hit it off the first time I stumbled in, asking for whatever the most New York breakfast item was, only for her to talk me into their blueberry bagel, which I absolutely loved.

Apparently, it's not a normal flavor for a traditional shop. Carl wanted to discontinue it, but she persuaded him to make a small batch every Friday for her and me.

Really, I had no choice but to enjoy the special treatment and let them enable my vice.

Even though there are millions of places to eat around this city, not to mention a few more convenient options on the way to the Q train, I'm a loyal customer.

He hands me a bag with the CARL COFFEE & BAGEL logo stamped on it, and I don't make a fuss over how endearing it is that he had my order queued up for me.

It even makes me feel like I belong here—for a little while, at least.

"Thanks," I say, dropping my cash on the counter. "See you next week!"

He rolls his eyes and focuses on the customer behind me. "What can I get you?"

I step out of the way and pull my phone out of my pocket, cueing up the camera to take a picture of myself smiling with ultra-serious Carl, knowing Angela and Mary will both get a kick out of it.

"Smile!" I call out, then click the camera button as he glares at me.

When I send the picture, both women react as expected, sending laughing face emojis.

I exit with a grin on my face and take massive bites of my prize as I walk to the park that overlooks the East River.

I've already read about the history of this area, along with the historic Gracie Mansion that I hope to tour someday, but I still open my phone and go down a Wikipedia rabbit hole, soaking up any information that I might have missed.

One of the many things I love about living here is the history and how thoroughly it's documented.

Most people in life want to pave a path for themselves, but every step in this city is one that has been taken thousands of times before. It helps me feel connected to millions of beating hearts—and generally less alone.

I'm desperate to find my place here, which is why I don't mind being a creature of habit.

Usually after my carbohydrate binge and stroll in the park, I take the train to a random stop. From there, I walk as far as I can, looking up facts about the areas I'm in to explore history as I experience it. I continue until my legs give out or I need to pick up Will from school.

All it takes is a few stops of the train to go from a swanky, mostly quiet part of the Upper East Side to the absolute chaos of the rest of Manhattan. I've been trying to get Peter and Amanda to let me take Will on a little field trip to anywhere outside this rich bubble of our neighborhood, but they're so overbearing that they shoot me down every single time.

It shouldn't come as a surprise, given that they've hired a full-time, live-in nanny to look after a teenager, but it does.

Will is a little small for his age, and even more sheltered, and I can't decide if his fragility is because of his half-dozen allergies, which they made me memorize on my first day—peanuts, shellfish, dust, pollen, cat hair, penicillin—or Peter and Amanda.

During the summer, I saw glimpses of Will's personality, usually after we spent an afternoon taking the long way home from his piano lesson or the nights we stayed in to watch movies while his parents were out. Now that school is back in session, he's getting eaten up by typical middle school politics and cruelty for being scrawny and shy, and I worry about him.

It's odd that his parents somehow manage to helicopter over him while spending as much time as possible actually not paying attention to him—like they just want to micromanage from the sidelines.

And that's why I don't really complain about spending so much time with him. I think he needs a friend more than anything else.

I finish up my bagel, then stroll along the windy promenade, trying to decide my course of action for the day. I mentally recite the stops along the train line, recalling all the stops and stations I've walked through to figure out if I want to repeat a favorite instead of exploring somewhere new.

I'm weighing the merits of all the options, so lost in my own head that I don't even realize the person walking in front of me has stopped until I slam right into him.

I jump back and hold up my hands. "Oh, I'm so—"

"What the hell is wrong with you?" he snaps.

My apology dies on my lips, stunned into silence at his anger.

His jaw is clenched, emphasizing the sharpness of its line and bringing my focus to the narrowness of his eyes and the creases on his forehead.

And he's looking at me like he actually expects me to answer that question.

"Um, w-what?" I stutter, blinking rapidly to take him in.

If his eyes weren't so full of hatred, I'd allow myself to appreciate his gorgeousness as he runs a frustrated hand through his shaggy blond hair.

"You know what you're doing," the man practically growls.

"I don't," I say cautiously. "But I'm leaving."

I back away slowly with my hands still in their defensive position.

The emotion on my face jars him into softening his posture, like he realizes he was being a total asshole for a simple mistake.

"Wait," he says.

I should channel my inner wannabe New Yorker and run like hell, but my feet are firm on the ground as I watch his expression transform from anger to panic.

My mind decides that it's because he's the type of guy

who doesn't let his temper get the best of him, and he already wants to backtrack.

Whether this is actually true…I guess I'm going to find out. I'm locked in some staring standoff with him, waiting to see what he'll do next.

"I'm sorry for snapping, it's just, today is…" He stops and clears his throat. "Look, for one day, all I want is a moment of peace in my own neighborhood without someone taking my photo or following me."

"You think I'm following you?" I ask incredulously.

He gestures toward the park entrance, and it's then I notice he's holding a Carl's cup in his hand.

"You stood outside my building, then followed me to my coffee shop and took a picture—"

"*Your* coffee shop?" I laugh at the audacity of a stranger to think he owns even one part of my Friday routine. "It's *my* bagel shop."

"I'll sign anything you want," he presses, not even bothering to argue with me over false ownership of Carl's place.

I laugh in disbelief. "I think there's been some sort of misunderstanding."

My words fall flat because he's not even listening to me speak them—he's busy glancing around, as if he's expecting a horde of people to be following him.

I sigh and take another step back, letting my eyes run over him from head to toe. Of course the sexiest man I've ever seen on the planet is some sort of paranoid, angry weirdo in the park, making wild demands about paperwork.

But no matter how easy he is on the eyes, I need to stay practical and safe.

My parents have lectured me a few times about carrying pepper spray with me around the city, but I've always laughed that idea off. Now, I'm wishing I had taken up their suggestion just to feel somewhat in control of this situation.

"I'm just, uh, going to go," I tell him.

He eyes me curiously as I back away, then once I'm safely behind a fence and a few benches, I turn and run—well, in my case, it's more of a fast walk—to the train and try to shake it off.

TWO

I shouldn't let one strange encounter get to me.

There are millions of people in the five boroughs, and I'm well aware of the fact that not every interaction I have is going to be positive.

I've grown slightly accustomed to people being annoyed that I'm too chatty or accidentally in their personal space on the train, but the fact that a man thought I followed him for blocks to take his picture...I'm not having an easy time letting go of it.

There was something oddly personal about the exchange. It was an accusation against my own personal character and integrity, and I can't let go of the nagging feeling that I should have explained myself.

It's stupid on a number of levels.

But given that I have no other real mental stimulation, I'm still fixated on it.

I stand in the kitchen, a little on edge, as I pour my cereal into a bowl.

Angela and I practically grew up on off-brand bags of Lucky Charms, but the only appealing thing I can find in this kitchen to eat in the morning is this organic, crunchy grain-free cereal. It's ridiculous that this is considered healthy by my standards because it's a far cry from the eggs, vegetables, and perfectly portioned potatoes that Amanda and Peter arrange on photo-worthy plates.

Even worse, even though my back is to him, I can *feel* Peter's eyes on me as he talks to Will at the table.

I shiver uncomfortably, wondering if I somehow made the stranger from yesterday feel this way—an invasion of privacy from a distance.

Up until I moved into the small third bedroom in the Finch family apartment, I lived with my parents in the small colonial home in a suburb. After years of living in cozy quarters with my sister and parents, this was an adjustment for many reasons, and at first, I didn't give any thought to wearing my pajamas while I ate breakfast.

It wasn't until Peter leered at me in my strappy tank top and sleep shorts that I realized my mistake of being just a little too comfortable. Since then, I have always made it a point to come out fully dressed and ready for the day.

"Good morning, Julianna," Peter says, bringing his cleared plate in to load into the dishwasher.

I smile politely and smooth down my long brown hair, shielding myself from him just a bit. "Good morning."

"Did you sleep well?"

It's such an innocent question, but whenever he asks it, I feel like I need to go take a shower.

It might be because it's accompanied by the strong, oaky scent of his cologne overtaking my senses.

"Yes." I swallow, not meeting his eyes. "Thank you."

I always try to answer him with as few words as possible without coming across as rude, but I generally prefer not to interact with him.

There's an overall skeeviness to him, and although there's no real outward indicator of this other than my observations and inferences, something deep in my gut tells me to keep my distance.

I'm very grateful to have this job, not to mention food and housing at no cost in New York, but I can't say that living with these people, taking care of a teenager and the obscene number of houseplants, is what I hoped I would be doing for the long-term.

My parents always encourage me to go for what makes me happy and not chase dollar signs like they've had to do for so long. I can't say at this exact moment that I am proud of all the years I paid universities to let me soak up everything I could under the direction of professors.

Getting my bachelor's degree in history was pure passion, and though I realized I had a nearly impossible chance at finding a job that interested me, I continued on, earning my master's and accruing a metric ton of student debt.

With that big number I owe the government and private lenders, there would have been no way for me to afford the move here and cost of living without moving in with the Finches. Even if I eventually find something in my direct field, I'll need to find my own housing and muster up the courage to survive on ramen noodles.

So, for now, I'm hoarding my spending money to save up for when that hopefully happens. My only splurges are

Bagel Friday and a Metrocard, and even then, I count those as absolute necessities instead of indulgences.

"So, now that you've been here a few months, you think you've settled in?" Peter drawls.

I can't tell if he thinks I'm acting entitled or if he's curious about whether I plan on staying for the long haul.

"I think so," I say lightly. "At the very least, I have mine and Will's routine down, which is the most important thing."

"That's good."

I nod. "Yeah."

"Well, is there anything at all you need from me?" Peter asks, fixing another cup of coffee for himself.

He and Amanda have been generous, setting me up with comforts in my bedroom and private en suite bathroom—a luxury I didn't even have with my own family—which is more than I could ask for but is definitely not what he's referencing.

"No, thanks," I tell him, picking up my bowl to join Will at the table.

I would definitely prefer to avoid mealtimes with the family, but one of the house rules is that I'm forbidden to have food in my room.

Bedbugs and cockroaches are something every single New Yorker worries about no matter how rich they are, apparently.

"Oh, good, you're all here," Amanda says, gaze flicking between Peter and me as she walks into the kitchen. "Julianna, we're going to need you to stay in with William again tonight. Peter, we've been invited to that private art event at the Met I mentioned earlier this week. The Danenbulls came down with food poisoning and offered us their spots."

She says this like I don't already stay in every Saturday night while they go to various fancy functions and dinners around the city.

"Okay," I agree.

"And if you could pick up Peter's dry cleaning on the way back from Will's piano lesson?"

"Of course."

"Also, I had that bag restitched at the tailor's," she continues. "They called to let me know that if I don't pick it up before four o'clock today, I can't get it until Monday."

I nod, adding it to my mental to-do list.

Will escapes to his room, leaving me to recall just how many things they ask me to do that fall outside of the contract I signed. I'm able to contemplate this and finish my cereal alone since Amanda drags Peter to their bedroom to talk about "expectations" for the evening.

Eventually, I have to pull Will away from his video games for his piano lesson, and while he complies with my request easily, he doesn't seem happy about it until I promise that we can sneak some ice cream later.

If there's one thing Will dislikes more than being pulled away from his gaming chair on a weekend, it's his piano lessons.

"I want to quit," he tells me as we wait for the elevator down to the lobby.

I sigh. "I know."

He's told me this one hundred times, and he has pleaded his case to his parents even more than that, I'm sure, but they insist it's for his own good.

"It's just like when my parents forced me to take ballet when I was a kid," I say, trying to relate to him. "At the time, I thought it was the worst thing ever."

And it kind of was—I swear my pinky toes never recovered from being shoved into those awful shoes.

Fortunately, it was the first and last time they forced me to participate in organized activity, partly thanks to Angela's eagerness to try out every possible thing she could sign up for but mostly because I refused to budge from my favorite reading chair.

"But now, looking back, it wasn't so bad," I tell him, even though it's only half true. "I learned basic rhythm and movement and other stuff."

Will considers my argument. "What can I learn from piano that I can't learn from video games?"

"I guess you'll figure it out when you're older," I tell him.

I, personally, can't think of one single benefit, other than it gets him out of the house, which is something Amanda and Peter always seem desperate to do.

"But until then, at least we have mint chocolate chip to get us through it."

He smiles, slowly and without showing any teeth, but I take it as a good sign that he's not going to argue with me further.

Finally, the elevator door opens, and just as I'm about to step forward, a gigantic mass of fur leaps toward me.

I gasp and instinctively jump backward, pushing Will behind me as the dog continues to pull against his leash.

"Pancake! Down!"

The big fluffball obeys, sitting immediately before

glancing up at Will and me with the most innocent expression, tongue waggling.

"So sorry about that," the woman says, twisting the leash in her hand to renew her grip. "She loves to greet people in a way that people do not like to be greeted."

Will and I sidestep the dog, who sniffs us as we slide into the elevator.

"Pancake, come on."

Once again, she obeys, moving back inside the doors and sitting at our feet.

As the original surprise subsides, I can't help but hold out my hand for her.

Pancake makes a yelp of excitement, pressing her wet nose into my palm.

The woman smiles. "She likes you."

"What kind of dog is Pancake?" Will asks politely, still not comfortable enough to let the dog do anything other than sniff his shoes.

"A Newfoundland," the woman says. "Which was all well and good when we adopted her while at the house in Connecticut, but now that we're here again, I'm very aware of how much we miss all the damn space. Not that our place here is tiny...I mean, hell, it's actually probably the same layout as yours. But this dog needs a room all on her own. Big diva over here."

Her constant rambling and toothy smile reminds me of Angela.

But where my sister is no-frills, this woman is pristine. Even with her shaggy companion, there's not one dog hair that I can see on her all-black outfit, and her white-blonde hair looks like it was just blown out at a salon.

"I'm Zoe," she says.

"Julianna," I tell her, then nod to the teenager beside me. "And this is Will. We live on fourteen. Obviously."

She nods. "Pancake and I are staying with my older brother up on twenty."

The door opens, and Pancake bolts through the lobby, dragging Zoe along behind her.

"See you around!" she calls over her shoulder.

"I guess it's a good thing I'm not allergic to dogs," Will says as we walk toward his piano lesson.

It's in another high-rise building, not too far from ours, and, apparently, his instructor is some world class pianist.

I used to go in with him and listen to him play, but the constant berating from his middle-aged teacher about his posture and missed notes grated at my temper, so now, I do a few laps around the block for the hour I wait.

It's a good thing kids are resilient at that age—or maybe it's just that Will's a good one—because in my retelling of my ballet lessons, I didn't mention the complete meltdown I had one day when I stormed out of class and threw my shoes in the dumpster. My dad was furious that he had to fish them out but accepted my show of quitting.

Luckily, they'd lost the garbage smell by the time Angela put them on a year later.

I smile at the memory as I stroll, noticing that some stores and townhouses in the area have put up fall decorations, and snap a few pictures to send to Angela.

This summer was a little brutal for a few weeks, so I'm grateful for the cooler weather and less pungent smell of hot garbage on the streets. I'm a little nervous as to how winter is going to impact my walking plans, but I can't wait to see how the city looks at Christmas.

As I idle at a crosswalk, waiting for the signal to turn, my breath catches in my throat—right in front of me are the same bright blue eyes that were narrowed in anger at me yesterday.

I force a blink, upping my confidence at the idea that my brain isn't tricking me, and I realize, it's *him*.

Only now, he's not standing in front of me in fury, but he's captured in a photograph—a cologne ad on the top of a yellow cab.

He's shirtless, leaning back on some beach, and smiling up at the sun. There's not even a cologne bottle to be found in the photo, but the image is clearly meant to entice people to buy the product, as if they would look and feel as joyous as him if they wore it.

With shaky hands, I pull out my phone and flip through my camera roll.

Sure enough, he's in the selfie I took with Carl—seeming equally annoyed—and in another photo I took on a random street, I can make out the definitive shade of his blond hair in the background.

"Oh no," I mutter.

I didn't recognize him in the park, but I connect the dots of who he is just fine as I search out the cologne brand online.

He's Gabe King—an actor, model, animal activist, according to a short bio I stumble across.

And while he hasn't been in anything I've seen, I am impressed by the list of films and television shows on his IMDb page. I banned myself from that site long ago, because although I am kind of a vacuum when it comes to learning, I find fictional stuff to be overwhelming.

In my spare time, I tend to watch documentaries or the History Channel, whereas Gabe's career ignited when he starred in a five-movie series based on some fantasy books that were crazy popular when I was a kid—I'm pretty sure Angela was obsessed with them for a while.

Since then, it seems like he's been bouncing back and forth between indie movies and big action flicks.

Professional career aside, he has an enormous, cult-like following on blogs and social media.

There are pages of paparazzi photos and a frightening number of clearly manipulated images of him with fans or the love interest from the fantasy series, Melanie Sonte.

People either seem to want him with her or want him for themselves.

I don't know how much money I'd be willing to trade for a total invasion of my privacy like he suffers, especially after seeing his reaction yesterday.

If my face were stitched onto random people's family pictures like it was nothing, I'd probably crave to be normal and anonymous, too.

The alarm on my phone goes off, my reminder that I need to turn back and pick up Will, and I do just that, hoping I don't see another reminder of Gabe and my misjudgment.

THREE

By the time Bagel Friday rolls around, I'm hopeful that I'll run into him again.

Given the millions of people who live in Manhattan, not to mention the endless possibilities of routes and the fact he might not be on my timetable, I know the odds are against me.

I'm partly ashamed of myself for letting myself get so fixated on our interaction.

It makes me feel like I'm just as bad as his fanatics—who call themselves "Commoners" in reference to his last name being King—because I've thought about him way more than I should.

Although I didn't get around to watching any of his actual performances, I went on a pretty serious binge of his interviews over the years, ranging from his original press conferences for the series that started his career, some backstage soundbites from modeling events, and even a few speeches he has given on behalf of a few animal rights organizations.

Gabe King can be a little self-deprecating, charming, or even confident as hell when he wants to be. Regardless of what front he's putting up, I think I get glimpses of the *real* him.

It usually happens for a fraction of a second, between questions onstage at conventions or while being shouted at in the middle of the airport, but it's clear that his face falls, like he's struggling to hold up the defense that shields him from the demands of the people speaking—or in most cases, yelling—to him.

It seems taxing for him to be so *on* for the crowd, which makes sense that he practically was on his knees begging me to leave him alone last week.

My mind did an adequate job of filling in some imaginary, troubled backstory and his inner thoughts, but after losing sleep to my own speculation, I've forbidden myself from any additional snooping online.

My habits may be pretty benign, but there's something gross about deep-diving into someone's life when I don't actually know who they are.

I've tried to redirect my curiosity into other topics like the state of our oceans and the process of how saltwater taffy is made—anything to keep my mind occupied while enduring the mindless work of chores. As a bonus, Amanda is very pleased by my renewed interest in her routine of caring for her houseplants, telling me for the sixth time all of their names and where she got them.

But now, I'm back in the park, sinking my teeth into my

bagel and trying to not let thoughts of him overtake everything else.

I force myself to have a little quiet moment, appreciating that for the next few hours, I don't have to do Amanda's bidding, avoid Peter, or attempt to not be the world's worst influence on Will.

Usually, I stare at the people milling about, but today, I take a deep breath and keep my gaze fixed on the gently moving water of the East River. It has a somewhat brown tint, which means it's not exactly the most romantic body of water to gaze at, but there are a few brave jet skiers and boaters speeding across it.

"Julianna?" a feminine voice calls out from behind me.

I turn to see Zoe, the woman from the elevator, heading toward me.

"I thought that was you," she says, stepping up to greet me like we're old friends.

I return her hug, then slyly try to wipe the cream cheese from my lips with the back of my hand, silently cursing Carl for cheaping out and not giving me a napkin this morning.

"How are you?" I ask brightly. "And where's Pancake?"

"I'm good, but it's mostly because Pancake is at doggy day care. It's actually kind of ridiculous because it's set up like some kind of dog spa. She's going to be groomed and spoiled all day, and I'm...also off to get groomed and spoiled all day."

We both laugh at that, and warmth spreads throughout my chest.

It's been months since I've had a conversation that

brought about mutual giggles. As much as I enjoy exploring the city on my own, it would be nice to make a real friend here.

"What are your plans today?" Zoe asks, reading my mind.

"I haven't decided yet," I tell her. "I have most of every Friday off from work, so I usually get a bagel and come here, then decide what random stop I want to get off on the subway, then explore for a while. I moved here in June, so I'm still getting my bearings in the city."

Zoe smiles. "Well, I'll bet that has helped you learn your way around really quickly."

"I've gotten lost every single time," I admit. "But it's been nice, and it helps burn off the bagel."

She laughs, then takes a pull from her vape pen.

I thought the marshmallow scent was some sort of oil-based perfume, but it's stuck to her and the air she breathes in and out.

Damn vices.

"Have you been down to Union Square yet?" Zoe asks, releasing the rest of her scented air downwind.

I tuck my hair behind my ear, trying to visualize it on the map. "That's the park with the arch, right?"

She shakes her head. "It's a few stops before it. Oh my god, if you haven't been, we have to go! It's Friday, so the farmers market is in full swing, and there is this carrot muffin that I'm absolutely obsessed with. And the noodle place."

I can't help but grin at her excitement.

"Oh, sorry," she says, realizing how she went from zero

to intruding on my life. "Is it weird that I just inserted myself into your plans?"

"Maybe," I say, letting my smile shine through. "But I'm game."

She claps her hands together excitedly. "Great, we just have to wait for my brother to—"

"Zoe?"

The deep baritone voice brings about completely different reactions from us.

Zoe is all smiles while she bounces on her toes, and my eyes bug out in surprise as she slips her arm through his.

"Gabe, this is Julianna," she says proudly, gesturing to me. "She lives in our building."

"Nice to meet you," I say, holding out my hand as Zoe takes another pull from her vape.

He sucks in his bottom lip at me, like he's trying to decide if I'm some super stalker who tracked down his sister to get in with him.

Enough time passes without him returning the gesture that I let my arm fall back to my side.

"How'd you two meet?" Gabe asks skeptically.

She balks at his attitude. "Why are you being rude?"

The smoke coming out of her mouth and nose makes her look like a cartoon bull.

I know exactly why, of course, so I try to breeze past it and answer his question directly. "We met in the elevator last weekend," I explain to him.

"Yeah?" Gabe says, guard up and perfectly intact.

"I'm the live-in nanny for the Finches." I doubt he knows who they are, but I think the more details I can give him the better. "Will and I were on the way to his piano lesson when we met Zoe and Pancake."

"Oh," he says, relief evident in his features.

Zoe lifts her eyebrows, silently signaling to me that her brother is acting like a crazy person, and continues on. "*Anyway*, Gabe can drop us off in Union Square on the way to whatever meetings he has today."

"I can?" Gabe deadpans.

"What is with you today? Stop being such a brat." Zoe shakes her head at him, then loops her arm through mine. "Come on, Julianna."

As she tugs me along, she mutters apologies for his behavior while I scarf down the rest of my bagel.

The door to the black SUV is held open by a driver, who actually *tips his hat* to us, like I'm in some kind of alternate reality.

Zoe informs him of the change in travel plans while Gabe slides into the front seat, and then we're off, speeding down Second Avenue.

Despite the pristine leather interior, it's not exactly a comfortable ride because I can feel the tension radiating from Gabe.

Or maybe I'm imagining it completely and projecting my own nervousness at the turn of events.

"So, I think we should start by getting my favorite apple cider from this little farm vendor," Zoe says.

I try to match her enthusiasm. "That sounds great."

"And then after that, we'll—oh god, Gabe, not the fucking spearmint gum."

Gabe ignores her as he unwraps a piece and pops it into his mouth.

She sighs and rolls her eyes like he can't be helped.

"Is there something wrong with spearmint gum?" I ask tentatively.

"It's this whole thing on the internet. When Gabe was, like, eleven, he was at some big press event—"

"It was ComicCon," he supplies, offering both of us a piece before he slips the pack back in his pocket.

"Yeah," Zoe continues. "All the adults in the cast were being super serious and normal, answering questions, and Gabe, apparently, was so over it, he started blowing these massive bubbles with a wad of gum, and it sparked this whole frenzy of obsessions from fans."

"Now, I've got enough spearmint gum to last me the next decade," Gabe says, his tone light and bored.

I slide the green stick into my mouth. "Right."

"Gabe's an actor," Zoe clarifies. "In case you didn't recognize him."

He glances back at me over his shoulder with somewhat of a challenging look.

"I didn't at first," I admit, hoping he understands that I mean from our first true interaction last week and not five minutes ago.

I turn away from Gabe, faltering under his scrutiny, only to have a cab pull up beside us, which makes me believe I'm destined to never escape this man.

"But the advertisements clued me in," I say, knocking my knuckle against the window.

"'A Royal Scent by Gabe King,'" Zoe says in a singsong voice.

Gabe groans and slides down in his seat, unable to bear seeing his own face staring back at him.

Zoe rolls her eyes. "It's not that bad, really. The spearmint oil is a little too strong for my preferences, but people went crazy for it."

"Well, if I had known I'd have to look at myself every time I tried to hail a cab, I wouldn't have let Rina talk me into it."

"As opposed to every single time you turn on the television?"

Gabe sighs. "Touché."

"Don't pity him," Zoe says to me, seeing my frown. "He's used to all the attention by now and gets just as many benefits as he does annoyances, I promise you."

I nod, unsure how to respond.

Distracting myself from the silence that has settled over us, I pull out my phone to take pictures out the window, but after I snap the first one, I see how darkly the windows are tinted. Plus, everything's a little blurry, and I'm sure Angela will be curious as to why I'm in a car instead of fighting for space on a crowded train.

"We can ask to pull over if you want," Zoe offers, watching me give up on the endeavor.

"That's okay," I say. "Thanks, though. They're just for my sister, and she's used to getting my low-quality photos."

Zoe smiles. "Does she live…sorry, where did you say you're from?"

"The exotic and beautiful Columbus, Ohio," I drawl. "She's in her last year of school and is bored out of her mind living at home, so I send her as many pictures as I can throughout the day."

"She doesn't get jealous?"

"No, she says the fact that I live a lame life in such a cool city makes her feel better about her own circumstances, even if I'm not really doing anything exciting."

Zoe snorts.

"Trust me, being a nanny is just as glamorous as it sounds," I continue. "Lots of errands and chores and homework. It's actually kind of like being back in school, only eighth grade math is harder than earning my master's degree."

"What did you study?" Zoe asks.

We keep up our conversation easily as we make our way down to Union Square.

I don't miss the way Gabe glances at me occasionally—either over his shoulder or in the rearview mirror—but Zoe holds my attention.

She asks me about all the places I've seen so far in New York, then makes me pull out my phone again so I can start bookmarking landmarks and restaurants she likes on my maps app.

I'm pleasantly surprised that her preferences aren't completely out of my price range.

"Left or right side?" the driver asks.

"Right, please," Zoe answers without even looking up.

It seems like once New York culture is ingrained in a person, mastering the layouts and most efficient spots to get dropped off becomes second nature. Last week, I was just impressed I managed to pick the right train car to drop me off at a familiar station exit instead of having to walk all the way down the platform.

When the driver pulls over, I barely have time to thank him before Zoe drags me out of the car.

And the rest of the day continues on like that, getting caught up in her enthusiasm for life, for spending money, and for showing me around.

We start by wandering through the farmers market, sampling fresh honey, locally grown apples, and cider. The carrot muffin she mentioned was a little too savory for my taste buds, but I pretend to love it.

Then she shows me some of her favorite stores, where I admire everything but don't dare break my budget by buying anything.

We walk up to the Flatiron Building, which I've never seen in person but know many historical details about, and then back down to her favorite noodle shop, where she insists on treating me to a bowl of chicken udon that's bigger than my head.

After lunch, we part ways.

We're both a little reluctant to do so, but she has a facial appointment at a salon in SoHo, and I want to walk for a bit before I pick up Will from school.

As I'm hitting my stride, my phone buzzes with a new text message.

Oh! Send me those pictures, will you?

After the third selfie I took for Angela, Zoe insisted that she should be included in my day's representation, so now I have a bunch of photos of us laughing and standing in ridiculous poses.

I send a batch that I know Zoe wanted to use for her social media profiles, then smile to myself at today's turn of events.

After spending the last week consumed by silly regret

and thoughts of Gabe, I feel lighter at somewhat smoothing things over.

I didn't bother telling Zoe about the first run-in with her brother—something I wrestled with all day—but she mentioned that he'd be busy with filming again in a few weeks.

Even if my friendship with his sister continues growing, I doubt I'll see him again anytime soon.

FOUR

My dad calls me as I weave my way up toward Will's school, wanting to catch up with me even though I know Angela shows him most, if not all, of the pictures I send.

He rants at me for a solid five minutes about some new diet my mom has him on to lower his cholesterol, letting it slip that he still goes for a bacon, egg, and cheese sandwich from the drive-through several times a week.

"Don't tell your mother, though," he says. "She'll kill me."

"Or she'll just give up and let your bad cholesterol give you a heart attack."

His deep chuckle makes me smile, but it falters when I get to the entrance of Will's school.

Usually, he's bouncing off the walls with excitement on Fridays, eager to have a weekend at home and not in his uniform, but now, he's standing off to the side, leaning against the building, with his arms crossed over his chest.

As I get closer, I can see the red rimming his eyes beneath his glasses, along with flared nostrils that tell me he's been holding his emotions in as best he can.

"Dad, I have to go," I say. "Work stuff. I love you. Tell Mom I love her, too, okay?"

"Okay, Jules. Don't work too hard. And love you, too."

I end the call and shove the phone in my purse, giving my full attention to Will.

"Hey, buddy," I say, holding my hand out for a fist-bump. "Ready to go home?"

He pushes off the wall but doesn't say anything.

When Angela and I were kids, we blabbed all the details of our day to our parents without hesitation, but Will's not like that.

Also, I'm not his sibling, friend, or parent.

I mean, I'm barely qualified to be his nanny, but I'm just grateful that his parents were impressed enough with my education levels and letters of recommendation—which were intended for use in my actual field, not this—to overlook my lack of childcare experience.

And as nice as the relationship Will and I have built these past few months is, and as special of a kid I think he is, I can understand why he wouldn't be keen on sharing details with me.

He is a teenage boy, after all.

Still, as we make our way back to the Finch apartment, I debate whether to pry or just be a mute companion.

"Can we...not go home yet?" Will asks, finally breaking the silence.

His voice is thick with emotion, and it guts me completely.

"How about a walk?" I suggest.

He nods. "Sure."

We don't talk, but I think it's the best form of help I can offer at this moment—sometimes a person just needs someone by their side in silence.

After a few blocks, the splotchiness on his face has dissipated, and he seems generally less wound up.

"You okay to head back?" I ask.

I want to give him all the space he needs to collect himself enough to face his overbearing parents without being picked apart, but I'm also conscious of what time it is.

"Yeah," Will says.

We pick up our paces slightly, and by the time we're in the elevator, we're both breathing a little harder than normal.

"Thanks, Julianna," Will whispers as the doors open.

"Of course," I say, unaware that the ride up is the last moment of peace I'll have with someone in the Finch family today.

"Where have you been?" Amanda shrieks as I open the door. "We've been worried sick."

Peter stands with his hands in his suit pockets, looking completely unbothered by his wife's agitation.

"When I call you, I expect you to pick up," she snaps.

She makes me feel like both Will and I are children in need of a scolding.

I've been an adult, responsible for my own well-being and finances, and I don't appreciate being spoken to like this.

I understand that I am her employee, but it doesn't

justify her behavior—coming home forty minutes later than usual is out of the norm, not the end of the world.

"We went for a walk to decompress from the school week," I begin to explain.

Amanda laughs sardonically. "To *decompress*? Because your lives are so difficult?"

I bite down on my bottom lip before my temper flares, letting her rant until I've composed myself enough to say as evenly as I can, "It won't happen again."

"Go to your room, Will," Amanda barks. "Julianna, you're dismissed for the night."

She waves me off and dramatically sighs at Peter, who follows her into the kitchen.

The smell of garlic and onions sizzling in preparation for dinner makes my stomach growl, but it's clear I'm on my own.

Instead of locking myself in my room, I head right back out into the hallway, needing some space.

I'm so irritated that I move on autopilot, taking the elevator down and walking briskly along the sidewalk, my feet carrying me all the way along my normal route to the park before I even realize what direction I've been going.

I claim a bench for myself, grateful that at this time of day right before rush hour, it's sparsely populated—I have it all to myself.

Just like Will needed a walk and a silent companion, I need a little safe haven where I can be alone.

Amanda and Peter have been good enough to me, but their emotions rule all our conversations. They seem to love being in control, especially of Will and me, which can't be healthy for anyone.

I get the feeling that Amanda, in particular, is deeply unhappy with her life, which is why she wants to micromanage Will—and, by default, me—so completely.

Judging by the conversations I've overheard, Amanda and Peter are both social climbers who are standing right at the edge of the in-crowd in whatever swanky New York circles exist.

Amanda's days are mostly focused on charity work, which should be a good thing, but I suspect she does it for show and not out of passion or altruism, while Peter rakes in a ton of cash in medical sales.

There's a hollowness in them that I've picked up on, and if there's one benefit to this situation, it's that I'm going to do everything I can to make sure something like that doesn't form within me—even if it means sweating this out for a year until I can follow my passion and get a new job and a place of my own.

"Hey, Julianna," a deep voice says, startling me.

For the second time today, Gabe catches me completely off guard.

I glance up at him, pleased to see that he looks entirely devoid of the skepticism and anger he felt toward me so recently.

"Hey," I say lightly.

He adjusts the hat on his head, attempting to cover more of the blond hair that sticks out on the edges.

My gaze is drawn to the flexing of his forearms and how the muscles are accentuated by the rolled-up sleeves of his shirt.

For the average passerby, I'm sure he looks like any

other attractive and successful guy, but when he faces me full-on, I nearly drown in the depth of his blue eyes.

"Can I sit with you?" Gabe asks, gesturing beside me.

"Sure," I say, sliding over and mentally scolding myself for gawking so obviously at him.

When he sits down beside me, he's close enough that I can smell the spearmint gum as he crackles it between his teeth.

Gabe rests his elbows on his knees and keeps his gaze outward toward the water.

Normally, I'm perfectly content to sit in silence, but something about his presence overwhelms me into nervousness, and I rack my brain for how to fill the void.

"Did you know that some people think Roosevelt Island is haunted?" I ask him, gesturing to the two miles of land across the water.

"I didn't," he admits.

"That building right there—" I point to the octagonal shape of the entrance. "—was once an insane asylum, but now it's luxury condos. And down toward the other end of the island, there's a crumbling building that was once a smallpox hospital. I've never been, but the pictures online make it look pretty creepy."

He gives me a sideways glance. "I thought your thesis was on transportation's impact on the middle class over the past two hundred years?"

My heart flutters at his retention of my earlier conversation with Zoe.

"It was," I say, impressed. "But I spend a lot of time in this park...and I got curious one day, so I looked it up. It's kind of..."

"What?"

"Lame."

He shakes his head. "I disagree."

I chew on my bottom lip and stare out at the water again, trying to come off as relaxed and cool, not the fidgeting mess that I currently am deep down.

Gabe clears his throat. "Anyway, I was hoping you'd be here because I wanted to apologize. I'm sorry about earlier."

"Just earlier?" I retort, surprising myself with my boldness.

He chuckles and leans back. "And last week, too. I promise I'm not always an asshole. It was just a bad day. Well, I guess it's a bad week, actually."

"I get it," I say.

His eyebrow ticks up like he doesn't believe me.

And he shouldn't.

"Well, I don't really," I admit, running a hand through my hair. "But I'm trying to empathize with you."

He nods. "I'll accept your empathy if you accept my apology."

"Done," I say immediately. "But I should also clarify something."

I pull out my phone and tilt it toward him, showing the pictures I've taken recently.

"I really didn't know who you were when we first met or that you were around while I was taking photos for Angela."

Gabe shrugs. "I'm familiar with having a very enthusiastic sister."

"Well, at least you have one who doesn't require a swath of pictures every time I hit up my bagel shop."

A smile tugs at the corner of Gabe's mouth, making me even more aware of his perfectly shaped lips and incredibly white teeth. "Don't you mean *my* coffee shop?"

I chuckle. "Maybe we should let Carl decide," I suggest. "After all, I've been going there religiously every Friday since I moved here, and you..."

"Try to go there as much as I can whenever I'm in New York."

"Well, not to brag, but Mary insists on keeping blueberry bagels on the menu partly because I like them."

Gabe's eyebrows pull together, and his mouth contorts in disgust. "What kind of person eats blueberry bagels?"

"The same kind of person who had no idea who you were until I saw your picture on an ad after we met, I guess," I say simply.

That makes him smile genuinely.

It's not lost on me what is happening right now.

In fact, as we banter back and forth, my inner self is screaming at the surrealness of the situation, but I stay grounded in the surfacing reminder that even though he has a massive fanbase and a recognizable face, at his core, he's just a guy.

A very, very, very attractive guy.

"So, you were telling my sister this morning about how you always wanted to live in New York?" Gabe recalls.

I nod. "I don't even know what started it, but for as long as I can remember, I've been obsessed with the idea of living here. It's kind of stupid, given that my other passion, history, doesn't exactly make it an affordable place, but I don't think I could ever picture myself trying to be, like, some sort of Wall Street finance bro."

"Do you want to work at a museum or something?" Gabe asks.

I shake my head. "I'm not really interested in it, and aside from that, it's really competitive, especially here. I'd be up against a lot more qualified art history majors who have likely spent years interning at relevant companies."

I stop, realizing I've been rambling, but he seems interested, so I continue.

"I think I could do really well as a research assistant for a publishing house, or maybe even a guest lecturer. I really should have had this more figured out before I spent years of my life in graduate school, then moved to a completely new place."

"No, it's kind of...refreshing, actually," Gabe admits. "I've met so many people over the years who have very specific goals and are really rigid about attaining them. Being driven is a good thing, but sacrificing all flexibility to go after a singular goal can be exhausting to the point of sacrificing enjoying your life."

"I like the way you put it," I tell him. "Do you think you can explain it to my parents for me?"

He shakes his head. "I barely convinced my own father that acting could be a career."

"But it worked out okay, right?"

"It looks that way now, but there were so many years of struggling to get to this point," he admits. "My mom was always my biggest cheerleader, though."

I see the heaviness make its way back into his features, like a weight dragging him down again.

"Zoe mentioned this morning that...it has been a year, right, since she passed? As of last week?" And then it hits me. "Oh."

I have immediate clarity on Gabe's attitude—well, not even that, but a little bit of an explanation on his mental state—and despite Zoe's insistence earlier, pity surfaces inside me.

He nods. "She loved this city. So it's good to be back here again, but—" He cuts himself off.

"But what?"

For some reason, Gabe's face is the pinnacle of regret, along with what I think is a little bit of shame. "I'm sorry."

"What are you sorry for?"

He runs a hand over his stubbled cheeks. "I have probably given you emotional whiplash."

"I think I'm surviving it just fine," I quip.

His chiseled features are jarring enough when he's closed off, but when he renews his gaze on me, there's no trepidation in sight, like he's cracked an opening into who he really is—and it's as terrifying as it is alluring.

It's not difficult to understand why he has such a cult following or why he protects himself so fiercely, but now that I've seen a glimpse of the layers buried beneath his exterior, my thoughts are consumed with how I can break down all the barriers.

I want to find the pieces of him that he doesn't share with anyone else.

"Gabe—" I start, not really sure what I even want to say, but I'm saved by his phone ringing.

He shifts slightly closer to me so he can retrieve it from his pocket, and I hold my breath, not wanting to be even more enticed by the spearmint scent.

"It's Zoe," he says as if he needs to explain why he's answering the call.

I try my best to shove down the deep desire that makes me want to pounce on him on this park bench—something that's incredibly out of character for me and surely an absolute no-no for someone who regularly has paparazzi following his every move—but it doesn't help that he doesn't retreat back to his side of the bench once he answers.

"Hey...no, I'm not home yet…because I'm not...I'm not being coy...I'm with Julianna at the park...yeah...okay, I will."

He turns to me while keeping the phone up to his ear, unaware that the metal arm of the bench digs into my side as I try to distance myself from him.

"My lovely sister forgot to invite you to a party that she is, apparently, throwing at my place tomorrow. Can you come?"

It's barely been twelve hours since I ran into Zoe in this very same park, and since then, I swear, I've felt every single emotion humanly possible.

Quickly, though, I realize that's a lie because for the first time since moving here, I've felt desire and longing in a way that I didn't even know was possible for me.

Still, I try to play it cool, pretending I have to think it over, like I have some sort of packed social calendar, but for once, I actually don't think that Amanda and Peter have roped me into staying in with Will.

I offer Gabe my slyest smile. "I think I can make it work."

FIVE

The next day, once my errands are finished, I'm not left with much time to get ready for the party.

Angela makes me send her pictures of possible outfits—I didn't exactly offer up all the details but she knows I'm going to a party—then texts me not to overthink running late because no one expects anyone to ever be on time, anyway.

But I strive for punctuality, not wanting to make a bad impression so early in my friendship with Zoe, so I move as fast as I can.

Somehow, I manage to shower, wash *and* blow-dry my hair, and pull myself together enough to show up only ten minutes late.

"I'm so glad you're here," Zoe says, pulling me by the wrist through the doorway.

I can barely take in the apartment because it's so packed with people.

I'm not sure if there is some sort of capacity guideline

or fire code for how much weight the floor can bear, but this is probably testing the limits.

Zoe clutches my arm desperately, weaving us through pockets of people I don't have time to acknowledge as we move down the hallway and toward the kitchen.

This apartment has the same setup as the Finches', down to identical marble countertops and stainless steel appliances, but it's littered with half-full bottles of alcohol and empty trays where I assume appetizers once sat.

Zoe inhales from her vape. "Don't tell Gabe I'm smoking in his apartment, but I'm stressed out and need the nicotine."

"There's a lot of people here," I say dumbly.

"Gabe's friend Josh brought friends over two hours ago so they could day drink before the party started," she says, miraculously not smudging one bit of her bright red lipstick as she takes another pull. "Bunch of fucking immature idiots."

"Well, this is for you," I tell her, handing over a bottle.

It seemed fancy in the store, but looking at the top-shelf brands of vodka right in front of me, this twenty-dollar bottle of wine is probably far below the budget she's accustomed to.

She thanks me anyway and rifles through the drawer until she locates the wine opener. As she works, she holds her vape pen between her lips, inhaling and exhaling the marshmallow smoke in short bursts.

I watch her nearly eviscerate the cork for a few minutes before I gently remove the bottle and opener from her hands.

"Here, let me do it," I suggest.

She steps back and takes a deep drag, holding it in her lungs.

"Sorry," she breathes, and the tension seems to dissipate into the air. "I'm used to boxed wine."

That surprises me. "Really?"

"I know," she says with a slight laugh. "I guess I never grew out of that phase in college, but I've kind of become a Franzia connoisseur. Remind me to make you my spiked cinnamon apple drink sometime when there aren't a bazillion people in the apartment."

She sets out two wine glasses as I pop the cork, then I make quick work of filling them to the brim.

"Cheers," she says brightly.

We both down our drinks in gulps—me out of nervousness, her out of exasperation.

"Gabe is going to kill me," she mutters, peeking around the corner. "He doesn't like to have people over as it is, and I barely convinced him to let me throw this *very* small party with only a few close friends, and now—"

"It's anything but that?" I prompt.

She laughs, then pinches the bridge of her nose. "And worse..." She lowers the volume of her voice. "It's all industry people."

"What does that mean?"

"That it's all the people he definitely doesn't want to have to talk to after spending an entire day shooting a magazine cover and being interviewed for a film he didn't even want to do in the first place."

"Oh." I consider her words. "He seems to, uh, have to do a lot of stuff he doesn't want to do."

Zoe snorts. "And that's after a successful fifteen-year

career. He has plenty of horror stories from his teenage years, back when all the studio execs owned his soul even more than they do now."

I hum. "I believe it."

Even being as disconnected from his world as I am, I can absolutely relate to bosses wanting to control your every move. It's unbelievably frustrating for me as a nanny, so I imagine it's undoubtedly one million times worse for him, living his life in the public eye.

The dull roar from the other room kicks up with a few cheers and excited greetings, and Zoe and I crane our necks to see Gabe walk in with a short, blonde woman trailing behind him.

"That's Rina, his publicist," Zoe explains. "She lives for this kind of shit."

She does look ecstatic at all the people here with their phones out and the attention being given to Gabe, which is a far different reaction than what is coming from the man himself.

For the group, Gabe is all smiles, making jokes about being unsure he walked into the right place, but when he sees Zoe—and, by default, me—his eyes narrow.

"Maybe we should infiltrate the group," Zoe suggests. "You know, have herd protection from his true feelings."

"I don't think I want to be associated with all of that," I say, glancing at some of the partygoers practically fighting for his attention.

Zoe snorts. "Plus, the alcohol would be lonely without us."

"Definitely," I say.

When we've nearly polished off the bottle of wine

between the two of us, Zoe and I are in fits of giggles, taking turns speculating on what exactly people are saying to him to win his attention.

Gabe finally makes his way into the kitchen, nostrils flared in agitation.

"Oh, hello, Gabriel," Zoe says lightly. "Lovely evening we're having, yes?"

Gabe snatches the wine glass from her hand and takes a generous sip. "I'm going to kill you, Zoe King."

"Don't blame me! I'm the one who wanted to go join you, but Julianna said no—"

"Hey," I protest, then fail to deliver any sort of rebuttal for myself.

"For future reference," Gabe starts, voice dropping low, "I'm always grateful to be rescued."

And damn if he doesn't say it like he wants me to be the one who saves him.

He barely has time to swallow down the remainder of the wine in Zoe's glass before people surround us in the kitchen.

Our safe haven has been infiltrated, and I'm roped into a conversation with a tall, middle-aged guy named Josh and eventually, Rina. She's one of those people who seems effortlessly chic, as if flat-brimmed hats and long, fake nails were made to be worn by her.

I'm wearing a bright blue, knee-length dress that's cinched at the waist. It's plain and comfortable, and it seemed flattering when I put it on.

But now that I can really see all the others dressed in immaculate clothes that seem to have been made specifically for them or tailored to perfection, I feel inadequate, even though I was super excited when Angela and I scored this dress on sale and off the rack last spring.

"So, what do you do?" Josh asks me.

"I'm a nanny," I tell him.

"Cool. For who?"

"The couple a few floors down."

He nods and takes a sip of his drink, gaze moving past me like he's trying to figure out who to talk to next.

"And what about you?" I ask politely.

"Set design," he answers. "But I've had a few cameos, too. Actually, remember the police detective who insults Gabe in the first *Eggy Smith* movie?"

The Adventures of Eggy Smith is the film series that essentially made Gabe's career as a teenager.

I never watched them in their entirety as a kid, and I have no plans to change that now as an adult.

Back then, I wasn't totally oblivious to the huge fandom around it, but I couldn't get into watching a kid solve crimes in the early 1900s, even if he was a vampire superhero.

"No," I admit.

"Oh," he says, surprised. "Well, that was me."

"You've never seen any of the *Eggy Smith* movies?" Zoe says with a chuckle.

I shake my head. "Well, I saw a few minutes of the first one when he's saving the girl from getting her purse stolen," I admit.

"That's the third one," Rina corrects me.

"Hilarious," Josh says coolly.

Gabe eyes me with renewed appreciation, though I can't tell if it's me or the wine I drank that makes me think that, so I pour the rest of the bottle into his glass, and he nods appreciatively.

"Did you grow up under a rock or something?" Josh asks.

"No," I say defensively.

"Then how did you *not* see them?" His tone isn't malicious, it's with bored interest, like I'm keeping him momentarily entertained.

I think I understand what Zoe means about "industry people."

I shrug, not wanting to offend Gabe or anyone else in the room. "Just wasn't my thing, I guess."

"You mean watching a young vampire superhero solve crimes that trained adults couldn't wasn't exactly mentally stimulating for you?" Zoe teases.

"Oh, come on," Josh insists. "I want to hear why you didn't like it. I mean, it's a classic."

Zoe rolls her eyes. "To you, maybe."

He laughs hollowly. "And to your brother, whose royalty checks have no doubt funded this wonderful party you've thrown."

For the first time I can recall, Zoe's expression darkens.

She looks like she's about to throw her drink at this guy's head, but she merely presses her lips together and shoots fire at him from her eyes.

"If it's any consolation, I'm actually kind of curious myself," Gabe says.

I sigh and start to explain myself. "Well, when I was a kid, my sister and I loved to window shop. Like, we'd make a whole day of it, walking around the mall and imagining owning all that stuff..."

I take another sip of wine, knowing that my next set of words is going to delight Zoe and irritate Josh, whose opinion I can't bring myself to care about.

"Anyway, we used to think Pottery Barn was the most magical store in the world, and there was this one vase that Angela was obsessed with. It was deep purple and had a crack in the center, and...it was in one of the scenes I saw. Kind of ruined it for me that a show set a hundred years ago, with all its costumes and historical representation, had something I could buy at the mall."

Both Gabe and Zoe burst out laughing, while Josh's expression darkens.

"Sorry," I say with a grimace.

Josh's jaw ticks, but he forces a tight smile. "It's...fine. I'm going to go catch up with Mary," he says before he makes a beeline back toward the living room.

"It's more than fine," Zoe insists once he's out of earshot. "I think you just made my whole entire year."

I give her a skeptical look as Gabe gets roped into conversation with various partygoers.

"Josh is the most pretentious person I have ever met in my life," she says, lowering her voice so only I can hear. "I don't even know why Gabe is friends with him still, honestly."

"Oh," I say because I don't know what else to say.

She sighs. "But a set designer's job is to make sure that nothing like that ever happens, let alone in a movie with that much of a cult following. If social media was as big back then, it'd probably be like when the Starbucks cup showed up in *Game of Thrones*."

"Right," I say, immediately feeling a little guilty. "Maybe I should go find him and apologize—"

I stop talking when my eye catches Rina's movements.

Her phone is at an odd angle, and it takes me a beat to realize she's trying to slyly capture photos of Gabe.

Just like during my binge of his interviews, I see how his face falls for a fraction every time someone gushes over him or asks a semi-inappropriate personal question, but he does his best to keep everything light and surface level, the persona of the perfect, likable guy.

As much as I don't like the idea of him—or anyone, really—being in pain, I'm kind of honored that I've gotten to see him a little off-kilter in the short time I've known him. It feels...more personal than all this glamour and falseness we're surrounded with here.

Of course, Rina only captures his best moments, tilting her phone to get Gabe's most flattering angles and make it appear as if he's cozying up with the women he's talking to now.

I feel like I'm getting a firsthand look at how rumors get spread on the internet.

I nudge Zoe with my elbow, then nod my head in the direction of the offending photoshoot that's taking place without anyone's consent.

"Rina, stop it," Zoe warns, batting her phone down. "You know Gabe's going to hate those."

She rolls her eyes. "If I don't take candid pictures of him, his social media feed would be mostly empty. Just posed ones of him and pictures of that damn dog."

"What's wrong with that?" Gabe asks, trying to force

himself out of his current conversation and into ours. "Everyone loves Pancake."

"Where is she at, anyway?" I ask Zoe.

"Hiding in my bedroom, probably," she answers, slipping her arm through mine. "Let's go check."

Gabe glares at Zoe, who is once again abandoning him, then gives me a pleading glance like my mere presence will make this situation better.

As thrilling as that realization is, I grimace before following her back down the hall to her room, and like Zoe predicted, Pancake is hiding under the bed, refusing to come out and socialize.

"Come on, Pancake," Zoe says, crouching down to entice her out.

I join her on the floor, resting my back against the dresser.

"Do you have any treats?" I ask. "The dog I had as a kid would do anything for food. It was the only way I could get him to not chase the squirrels in our backyard."

Zoe scoots back out and hands me a pouch from her dresser. "Good luck."

I create a trail of the bacon-scented circles from underneath the bed out toward my lap.

Pancake slowly but surely makes her way out, retreating a few times before she finally sprawls out, resting her head on my thigh so I can scratch behind her ears.

"You're a genius," Zoe beams.

I shrug. "I am also food-oriented and not very social, so I get it."

"Zoe," Gabe seethes as he stands in the doorframe,

wiping bright red lipstick off his cheek. "You know I can't kick all of these people out myself."

"Okay, okay, I'll fix this." She chews on her bottom lip as she thinks. "You two stay here, and I'll be the bad King who doesn't have to face leaks in the press."

"What are you going to do?" Gabe asks, crossing the room to sit beside Pancake, who wags her tail excitedly. "Cut the power?"

Zoe's eyes take on a devilish gleam. "Better. Cutting off the alcohol and hiding you should do it. Stay here until I come back."

I move to follow her, but she waves me off. "Someone has to keep the dog company," she says with a wink that doesn't go unnoticed by either Gabe or me, then shuts the door swiftly, as if her decree is resolute.

SIX

I would much rather be in a room with a dog than forced into conversations with other people, and I get the feeling Gabe shares this preference.

Once Zoe shuts us in, we don't flow into easy conversation because we're both focusing on Pancake, who is rolling around on her back in the middle of the carpet, begging to be scratched.

We both oblige her, laughing as she practically purrs at the attention, like she's a tiny house cat instead of a huge, fluffy dog.

"When I was in undergrad, they had this program during finals where the local shelter would bring in dogs for students to go play with," I tell him as I sit back. "Research shows that dog therapy can help with PTSD, panic attacks, and...nights following exceptionally long days when you just want to relax but a large party is being thrown in your house against your will."

Gabe laughs. "I can't say those are all on the same level, but who am I to argue with an academic?"

I smile at that, then again when Pancake rolls over to once more rest her face on my leg. "Good girl," I tell her, scratching right under her chin.

There's a loud *clunk* from the other room, quickly followed by the sound of glass breaking.

"I got it!" Zoe yells loud enough for both of us to hear it.

Gabe runs a hand through his hair, though I think he's more exhausted from the day than fazed by whatever just shattered.

"So, I'm guessing you don't throw parties often?" I venture.

"Definitely not."

"Poor Pancake doesn't like to have all these people in her space."

"I try to use her as an excuse to get out of many things, but, clearly, it fails." He exhales, tone turning somewhat serious. "I'm also never really in one place long enough to establish a home or people to host. I'm usually traveling for months at a time, shuffling between here and Los Angeles, or wherever I'm shooting, but I'm in New York for the rest of the year, which is long enough that Zoe wanted to come stay with me."

She implied over lunch yesterday that she's slightly embarrassed about her career as an influencer, given how successful her older brother is, but she can't decide what exactly she wants to do.

For now, she's content to peddle legging brands while

visiting her father in Connecticut, or Gabe wherever he's filming, or friends around the world.

Gabe clears his throat. "So…you've really never seen any of my work? Aside from that ten minutes of *Eggy Smith?*"

"I'm sorry," I say, a little embarrassed. "It's just not my thing."

"What do you mean?"

I chew on my bottom lip before I answer. "I don't like movies or television, really."

He blinks rapidly, clearly surprised by that admission. "Like, at all?"

"I think it's because I've only ever enjoyed reading nonfiction." I try to explain my personal brand of neuroticism as best I can. "I'm pretty sure I made it through every single memoir in our local library branch at home. My sister, of course, always wanted me to watch some teen drama or *Star Wars* movie with her, but...my brain tries to treat that kind of stuff as fact, so I tend to look for the flaws and poke holes in it."

"Which is why the purple vase stuck out to you," Gabe says, piecing it together.

I nod, then grin. "Well, as believable as you were as a teenage vampire, yes, that was what ultimately made me give up on it."

He laughs heartily.

"But I mostly watch documentaries when I do sit in front of the television…with all the commercials and options on streaming services, I get kind of overwhelmed with information. It's like my brain itches, and I need to know every single thing. I've even banned myself from IMDb."

He stares at me for a beat. "I've never met someone like you."

"I'm going to take that as a compliment," I tell him resolutely.

Gabe's phone buzzes enough times that I can hear it in his pocket.

"Ugh, it's Rina," he groans as he pulls it out. "She wants me to post one of these creepy pictures she took of me."

"They can't be that bad," I press.

"See for yourself."

He hands his phone over without hesitation, which is an immense signal of trust from anyone, let alone a celebrity with millions of followers.

I overheard a few girls earlier talking about him like he was some untouchable god, so high up on a pedestal that it would be an honor to claim him as a prize.

But here, on the floor of his sister's bedroom with a dog between us, he's just normal.

I mean, he's, like, *obscenely* attractive—it would do the world a disservice to not have his face plastered on billboards—but other than that, very much normal.

The photos Rina sent are, as expected, incredibly flattering.

They all catch him at just the right moment, smiling, laughing, or actively listening while taking a sip of wine, but there's something about them that doesn't seem genuine.

At least, not compared to now when he's relaxed on the floor with Pancake curled up next to him.

The versions of him in the photos are the ones the world expects—a perfect gentleman with a pristine reputation who is here to be stared at while entertaining the masses, the one who is forced into conversations and speculated about—but it's not *him*.

I'm getting the real Gabe King, right here in the flesh.

The rest is just for show.

I flip to his camera app and turn the screen so he can see it. "Can I?"

He quirks an eyebrow but doesn't deny my request.

I take a bunch of photos, wanting to document how I see him in this exact moment, relaxed and meeting my eyes.

I sit up, tucking my legs, so I can get a different angle, and snap a few more.

"I didn't take you for a paparazzi," he says lightly.

"I thought you'd be used to this by now."

He runs a hand through his hair, slightly messing up the way it was styled for the shoot. "There are some things that will forever be weird, and for me, posing is one of them."

"Well, it's a good thing you're not doing that now," I tell him. "You're just spending time with your neighbor and your dog."

He smiles up at me, and I take one final photo, then hand his phone back to him.

"Why can't you just use photos from the shoot today for your social media?" I ask curiously.

"There are all sorts of rights issues with the photographers, so they have to go through their process, and even if Rina took behind-the-scenes photos, they want us to time their release with the cover story coming out in January to get that extra promotion for it."

"That seems like a lot of coordination."

"It is. Going from one movie set to the next table read, the next fitting, the next forced personal magazine interview..." He grimaces and rights himself. "Sorry. It's embarrassing for me to complain."

"You shouldn't be embarrassed. This—" I gesture to myself, Pancake, and Zoe's chrome furniture. "—is a safe space to vent."

I see the consideration on his face as he wonders if my words are actually true.

Gabe sighs. "Have you ever had a feeling that what you've worked for isn't what you actually want?"

"Not in the way you have, I don't think," I admit. "But us mere mortals don't have the same kinds of problems you do. I get that everyone wants to have a rich and luxurious lifestyle, but they might not be aware of the negatives that come along with it. For example, I, personally, can't imagine the mental state of someone who thinks an innocent woman in the middle of her Bagel Friday routine is stalking him."

"Me neither," he drawls. "Sounds like that person should be avoided at all costs."

He laughs and reaches into his pocket for a pack of spearmint gum.

I'm not sure if it's habit or therapy for him at this point, but I enable it, taking a stick from him.

"I don't know how you do it," I murmur.

"Did you know that if you fake a laugh long enough, your real one comes out?" Gabe asks.

I chew through the first hard bites of gum until it becomes malleable. "Is that true?"

"Try it out," he encourages, raising a challenging eyebrow.

So I do.

At first, it feels awkward and forced, which makes me feel even more uncomfortable, so I laugh, and soon, it's real, then Gabe starts laughing at my surprise.

"Neat party trick," I say, still holding on to the remnants of my chuckle.

"I do what I can," Gabe says. "Want to help me pick out a photo for my feed?"

I scoot closer to him so we can scroll through the pictures together, and we narrow it down to either one that Rina took or the one I did.

"You don't like one better than the other?" Gabe asks curiously.

"You don't look hideous in either," I tease.

"Thank you for that ringing endorsement."

I shrug. "You can ask Zoe. She's the social media pro, after all."

"I've got it," he says, holding a hand over his screen while he posts.

I'm shielded from his decision, but he looks at me smugly once he's done.

"Well?" I ask. "Which one did you pick?"

"Look for yourself," he suggests.

I pull my phone out of my purse, then do a Google search to pull up his account.

"You're not even following me?" Gabe teases.

"I don't have any accounts," I tell him. "Part of the itchy brain thing...too much information."

"Wow," he breathes. "Lucky. Rina would skin me alive if I tried to take down my accounts. Or she'd just create her own for me, which would be way worse."

I snort as I ignore the prompts to download the app and click on the picture he posted. "You went with mine," I say excitedly.

I take in how beautiful he looks even in a relaxed pose on the floor.

He's still in his full photoshoot attire, but the moment I captured his attention, his gaze was off in the distance, just enough to come off as thoughtful or pensive.

Then I read the caption.

"'Thinking about purple vases,'" I read aloud, and this time, my laugh is very genuine.

"I'm no doubt already getting thousands of comments." He says those words not to brag but because they're true.

I take a few of them in one swipe, and I'm already overwhelmed. "This is...a lot."

"If I spend too much time on there, I feel like I'm drowning. I do try to have fun with it because I have to engage sometimes. Studios love it, and now, more often than not, there are specific promotion details written into my contract."

"There are, like, three marriage proposals right here, and I've only seen a handful of comments," I balk.

"Oh, that's tame stuff," he assures me. "I've had people legally change their names to characters from *Eggy Smith* or claim to be related to me. Every type of stalker in the world has come after me, so much so that I had to buy my house in Los Angeles through a shell company. Also, this one woman very painstakingly stitched my face into years' worth, and I mean *years'* worth, of family photos in an attempt to convince me that I belong with her."

"Wow," I breathe.

"I think even if I were to quit the business now, the harassment wouldn't stop," he says grimly. "It's gotten worse over the years, honestly. Especially every time Melanie or I promote a movie."

"Why's that?"

He smiles, reminding himself that I don't know all the details of his life like everyone else he's surrounded by does. "My friend Melanie played my love interest in *Eggy Smith*, and there has been fifteen years' worth of speculation on whether we're really together."

"Oh," I say.

"One time, my publicist came across a registry set up for us, and people had spent thousands on gifts, hoping to be invited to our fictitious wedding. I guess one good thing is that we donated everything to charity, but...to your point, it's just overwhelming sometimes."

"It sounds like it," I admit.

Zoe bursts through the door, and it startles me, Gabe, and Pancake enough that we all jump.

As grateful as I am to have my friend back, I like the little bubble Gabe and I have created in here, and I'm not ready to leave it.

"Well, that's it," she says proudly. "Everyone's gone, and the only casualty was one bottle of Angel's Envy."

"Not to mention the emotional scars I will now carry

with me at the thought of so many people being in my home," Gabe deadpans, but even he can't keep up his false anger.

Zoe ignores him and holds up her phone, showing him the picture he just posted.

"Cute, isn't it?" Gabe drawls.

"What's cuter is that now everyone is speculating on who the girl is in the photo."

"What?" Gabe and I say at the same time.

I pull up the picture once again, and it takes me a second—along with the zoom-in pinch of my fingers—to see my legs were captured in the photo, reflecting in Zoe's chrome-plated nightstand.

"I didn't even realize that," I say, horror-stricken, to Gabe. "I'm so sorry."

"What are you sorry for?" Zoe asks. "Your legs look fantastic."

"Isn't this going to cause some sort of PR issue?" I ask.

Gabe shrugs it off. "There's always some response every time I post, leave the house, or breathe. Rina will handle it."

"In the meantime," Zoe says. "We can plan for next weekend. Don't give me that look, Gabe. If it weren't for me, you'd go to work and then come home and do nothing, and while I'm here, that's not going to fly. Plus, I promised Rina that if she helped me get rid of everyone tonight, you'd make an effort at being social."

"Selling my soul to the devil," he mumbles.

She ignores him. "Obviously, Julianna, you *have* to come to Dream with us. It's this really cool nightclub downtown where we celebrated my twenty-first birthday last year, and from what I remember, we all had a blast."

"A nightclub isn't really my thing," I hedge.

"It's everyone's thing," she insists.

I turn to Gabe. "Does she ever take no for an answer?"

"If she does, I wouldn't know."

SEVEN

It turns out that I actually *am* able to say no to Zoe, but it's not exactly by choice.

Peter and Amanda are heading to some exclusive restaurant opening, so I'm stuck in for the night, hanging out with Will.

He is already glued to the television in his room, playing video games while I'm waiting for his parents to leave so I can listen to a true crime podcast that Angela recommended to me.

As I wait, I have to watch Amanda flit around and speculate about who is going to be there, how they can ignite friendships, and who they can network with, and it makes me feel ill.

Normally, I'm all for people branching out and making friends, but there's something grating about opportunistic people, as if they can only befriend someone to leverage themselves into something better. That doesn't sit right with me.

Maybe that's why I can't stop thinking about Gabe.

It's people like Amanda who want to use people to make their own situations better or more appealing to others, and it's exactly the type of behavior Gabe seems to try to avoid.

It seems like, aside from his sister, most of the people he is surrounded by are either his colleagues, people who want leverage to his stardom, or fans who desperately cling to his identity as Eggy Smith.

I picked all of that up at just one party, not to mention the amount of press coverage I've followed this week on "Gabe King's mysterious, long-legged lady."

I don't even think my legs are that long—they're skewed a bit in the photo thanks to the reflection in Zoe's nightstand—but it's all his fanbase seems to be able to obsess over.

Not only that, but I can see people tagging him and his former co-star Melanie in other photos, which have been manipulated to show unwavering fan support for the couple that has never actually been a real-life couple as far as I know.

But then again, what do I actually know?

I've spent more time thinking *about* Gabe King than I have actually spent *with* him, which makes me feel pretty embarrassed and ashamed of myself.

Instead of blaming the real culprit—my curious mind—I blame my circumstance.

My job is usually filled with many mindless hours, which isn't too terrible, but it's becoming all-consuming.

Or rather, Gabe King is.

I don't want to just be another admirer, one of the

millions lined up and vying for his attention. As appealing as his looks are—really, he's too gorgeous to exist in the same plane of existence as mere mortals like me—there's something deeper that draws me to him.

It's the desire to know what exists behind the front he puts up for everyone else.

"Is dinner almost ready?" Will calls from his bedroom now that we're alone.

His parents would definitely scold him for yelling in the apartment, but I can't bring myself to do it.

They expect him to act like a fully matured adult instead of a teenager, but I, for one, would have rather stuffed my face with pizza and ice cream at his age—an option that sounds really good right about now, considering I am a pretty terrible cook, but Amanda and Peter would kill me.

"Another five minutes," I yell back.

"Okay!"

I can hear the repeated clicking of whatever button he is pushing on his controller to fire his weapon in the video game he is playing.

Surprisingly, my aversion to television and movies doesn't apply to the war games he plays. I'm able to treat the sounds and dialogue as white noise when I sit in his room with him, and when I actively watch him play, there's something about controlling that false reality that appeals to me.

The doorbell rings, startling me from my place in front of the stove.

Usually, the concierge on the first floor will call to let us know a delivery is coming up for us, but I assume Peter and

Amanda are having too great a time schmoozing, or whatever it is they're doing, to give me a heads-up.

I turn the burner's knob to a low setting, cover the pan with a lid, then wipe my hands on a dishtowel before I open the door.

I'm expecting a delivery person in a uniform holding an oversized box, but instead, I get Gabe in dark, fitted jeans and a hoodie with a faded logo across the front of it.

Somehow, he looks even better in this than he does in a suit.

"Hi," I say, smoothing my hair down.

I didn't even check my reflection in the hallway mirror before I opened the door, so I hope and pray there aren't stray seasoning bits or pieces of vegetable on me.

"Hey," he replies, then traps the edge of his bottom lip between his teeth.

We stare at each other for a beat before I state the obvious. "You're not out with everyone else."

He shakes his head. "I faked a headache to get out of it."

"And Zoe bought that?"

"I am an *actor*, remember?" Gabe says with a smile. "But...no, not until I gave her my credit card. Whatever dent she puts in it with bottle service will be worth a few hours of peace."

I don't know what bottle service is, but it sounds expensive.

"So you'd rather spend your night standing in my doorway?" I ask slyly.

He runs a hand through his hair, letting his gaze falter for a moment before his eyes meet mine. "Yeah, well, it's one of my last Saturdays of freedom in pre-production, so I wanted to see if you wanted to...hang out?"

My heart pounds in my chest as the question hangs in the air.

For someone who is supposed to be a confident, womanizing, Hollywood-type, he's not projecting that vibe as he shoves his hands in his pockets.

Peter and Amanda would absolutely not be pleased about me having a guy I barely know over for the evening when I'm supposed to be focusing on Will—even if he is completely self-sufficient and not in need of a nanny.

Then again, maybe they'd be thrilled at the idea of having someone with Gabe's level of notoriety in their home.

"Well, I'm kind of working..." I falter.

His face falls. "Right," he says, backing out of the doorway. "I should have—"

"Julianna! I'm getting pretty hungry." Will sprints out of his room, then slides across the wood floor in his socks, barely stopping himself before crashing right into me.

His parents have told him at least twelve times in my presence to not do that because it makes the floor extra slick. I, however, never scold him for that—or anything, really.

I might be the world's worst and most useless nanny.

"Hi," Will says to Gabe. "Who are you?"

I can see the wheels turning, like he knows Gabe is familiar but can't place him. I honestly have no idea which of Gabe's projects would be appropriate for Will to see other than *Eggy Smith*, which was before his time.

"Gabe," he says, holding out a hand.

Will is too cute when he shakes it firmly, a move that I've seen Peter practice with him numerous times.

"Are you coming in?" Will asks.

Gabe looks to me for permission.

I shrug. "I'm just finishing dinner and then Will's going to teach me how to play the new *Call of Duty* game."

"Do you play?" Will asks Gabe excitedly.

"I did when it first came out," he admits, then he laughs. "Which was probably before you were born, now that I think about it."

"You're not *that* old," Will says.

Gabe holds his hand up to his chest like the teen has wounded him.

"Come on." I usher him in toward the kitchen, letting the front door slam shut, and both of them follow along.

Condensation drips down over the stir-fry when I lift the lid off the pot, and I grimace at the congealed mush that meets my eyes. Stirring doesn't help anything other than give me something to do while I curse myself internally for not being a better cook.

Gabe glances over my shoulder at the sad excuse for dinner. "We can save this," he says confidently.

"We can?" I ask, not believing him.

He nods, pushing up his sleeves. "Will, can you help me pick some spices out from the cabinet?"

All I can do is stand back and watch Gabe take charge in the kitchen, getting all the assistance he needs from Will.

They both pick out some jars of spices, then raid the fridge, looking for herbs and sauces.

"Even if the texture is weird, the flavor is what is

important," Gabe explains, sprinkling a little bit of each item they retrieved into the pan and stirring it together.

Will nods like he's in complete agreement with this and adding to my culinary education, and I have to bite back a smile.

Gabe scoops out a small spoonful, blows on it, and performs a taste test.

"Not bad now," he decides, offering the wooden spoon for Will to do the same. "What do you say?"

"Could use a little more salt, I think," Will says.

"Do it up," Gabe encourages, sliding the container over.

We both watch him pour too much salt over the meal, but when we serve ourselves, we end up clearing the pan with vigor, letting hunger overpower any pickiness.

Will chats animatedly with Gabe about school and video games, clearly happy to have someone other than his parents or people employed by them to talk to.

I wave them both into Will's room to get started on the game while I clean up dinner, then I spend the next two hours watching them yell at other people and wander around a desolate, pixelated landscape.

When my phone alarm goes off, my reminder that it's Will's bedtime, he immediately groans without even breaking his stare on the screen.

"Already, Julianna? Can't I stay up late with you guys?"

I shake my head. "If you don't start winding down now, you'll be wide awake when your parents get home. We both know that wouldn't be good for either of us."

One of the first weekends they went out, they came back a little early, which coordinated perfectly with the one time Will convinced me to let him stay up late. We both got scolded for our actions.

"I know," he grumbles. "But you'll come back, right, Gabe?"

Gabe smiles. "Sure thing. And we can play online, now that you guided me on what to get."

I don't expect him to actually go through with playing video games with a teenager like he says he will, but every single part of me hopes he does.

My heart hurts for how lonely Will is, and I can tell how much this night has meant to him.

After Will brushes his teeth and high-fives us both goodnight, I close the door to his bedroom and walk Gabe slowly back toward the front door.

"I'm afraid you didn't get the peaceful night you imagined," I say lightly.

"Not exactly," he says, but his smile widens. "But I still enjoyed it."

"Saving stir-fry and hanging out with a thirteen-year-old *does* sound more entertaining than some loud nightclub," I agree. "I mean, you got to kill bad guys and you still get to go to bed early. What could be better than that?"

"Definitely better than being photographed and yelled at all evening."

I frown. "Is it always like that for you?"

"Not always," he admits. "I do get some level of anonymity, and the club that Zoe likes does have a private room, but...I guess I'm not much for going out these days."

"I understand. I had a rebellious semester in college, and when I think back to how much cheap liquor I drank three nights a week..." I sigh. "This is better for my liver."

"You know," Gabe says. "I think you're the most down-to-earth person I've ever met."

"Is that another way of saying 'boring,' or are you complimenting me again?"

"Trying to."

He puts his hands in his pocket and leans on the wall beside the door, silently signaling he's not quite ready to leave yet—and I don't want him to, either.

I nod. "I guess it's not that difficult to come off as grounded compared to the people you usually hang out with."

"That's true," he allows. "But...I don't know. I don't think you give yourself enough credit."

I fidget under his appraisal of me—just because I scrutinize everything I see doesn't mean I want to be under a microscope myself.

"Well, I'm sorry to push you out like this, but I think the Finches will be home soon," I say as I open the door. "Thanks for saving dinner and helping me entertain Will."

It's a little embarrassing that I've reverted back to a teenager trying to get rid of her crush before her parents come home.

Gabe laughs. "He's a good kid. I'm definitely going to take him up on his recommendations and try to get a system set up in my trailer. Should help me kill some downtime."

I practically bounce with joy at that declaration, but I try to keep my cool like Gabe seems to be able to do most of the time.

Well, except for this exact moment because it seems like he's lingering in uncertainty.

In a moment of insanity, I decide to just go for it.

He made the first move in coming down here—something I have yet to truly process—so I suppose it's only fair that I open myself up to rejection this time.

"Do you want to do this again?" I ask him before I can think better of it. "Well, not *this* exactly, but...I don't know, maybe we could spend some time together next Saturday? If you're free?" I stop myself from rambling and feel the redness overtake my cheeks.

"I'd like that," Gabe says.

I smile. "Okay."

I grip the doorknob and wait for him to step outside or hug me or do something other than stare me down.

He raises his hand slowly, and I watch the movement as he lightly touches my cheek with the tips of his fingers, which sends a jolt of electricity down the entirety of my body.

"Good night, Julianna," he murmurs, then backs away down the hall.

I close the door and press my back against it, sliding to the floor while holding my palm up to my burning cheek.

EIGHT

I wake up the next morning a little groggy and completely twisted in the sheets.

If it's possible to be hungover from a cocktail of disbelief, excitement, and appreciation of a very attractive man, then that's what I am currently experiencing.

It doesn't help that Angela wakes me up with a phone call at seven a.m., only to begin babbling about some date she went on the night before that did not end like she hoped it would.

She fills me in on all the details, and I merely have to mutter, "Uh huh," every minute and a half to keep her going long enough for me to dress and slip out of my room to make a cup of coffee.

I'm not huge on caffeine because of all the mixed studies I've read on the long-term health impacts, but I'm desperate for it today.

It feels like an indulgence, sipping on the rich, hot

liquid that has a hint of hazelnut to it as I sit on the floor, resting my back against the bed as Angela drones on.

"...and so, at the end of the night, after all that, he just gives me a handshake," she says, seething. "Can you believe that? A *handshake*."

"Wait, what? After all the romantic stuff he said to you over chow mein? It just ended like that?"

"I know, right?" Angela sighs. "I swear I have swiped through every single guy within a twenty-mile radius of Columbus. You're so lucky to be in such a big city."

I scoff. "Right, because I have so much free time to date right now."

"That's on you, Jules," my sister scolds. "These people are taking total advantage of you. I mean, you work pretty much twenty-four seven, which is definitely some sort of violation."

"I'm aware of the labor laws in New York," I say evenly, not wanting to get lectured by my younger sister at all, let alone this early in the morning.

"Then you should stand up for yourself!" Her tone is more pleading than anything else. "Don't let them monopolize your time and force you to do housework when your contract explicitly states what they are and are not allowed to do. Set some boundaries and get more balance in your life."

"I don't mind doing it, Angela," I argue.

But she and I both know I'm lying.

I let out a breath. "I feel like I'm finally getting settled here, and I can't afford to lose this job."

"Said every person who has ever settled," Angela pipes in.

"The fact that I live here rent-free is huge," I press. "Even the cost of food here is absurd. I went to the grocery store the other day, and they were charging eighteen dollars for a carton of sliced pineapple. Insanity, right?"

"Wow," Angela says lifelessly. "You should definitely add that to your dating profiles."

I roll my eyes because joining one of those apps is one of the many things she would always try to get me to do while I still lived in Ohio. "You know I don't do any of that."

Angela laughs. "That doesn't mean I don't not get to tease you about it."

I feel the tension between my temples increase. "That doesn't make sense."

"Yes, it does," she argues.

"You tried a double negative but somehow triple negatived me."

"I know what I said."

"No, you—"

"Anyway," she cuts in. "Now, let's move on to the real reason I called."

I pinch the bridge of my nose with my thumb and pointer finger, then take a deep breath. I pull the phone away from my face to see that we've already been talking for forty-seven minutes, and we're apparently *just* getting into it.

"You mean you didn't specifically call me this early in the morning to completely rehash your date?" I ask her.

"I don't recall you being this difficult before you moved away," she snaps.

Angela and I have always had a combative yet loving

relationship, able to go from arguing with each other fiercely to crying in each other's arms within minutes.

I'm supposed to be the wiser and older sister, but I swear since the moment she was born, she's had this ferocity about her that has always made me consider her my equal.

More than that, really.

She's always the one who pushes me to go out and meet people and try new things, and she was the most vocal with excitement for me after I finally admitted my dream of moving to New York, which is why sending her regular updates is so special and fun.

Even when she annoys me, I can't help but love her wholly.

Angela clears her throat. "Dad's not doing that great."

"What?" I balk. "What do you mean? With work or health?"

"Both, I guess."

I set down my empty mug so I can rub my eyes, as if clearing my vision will help me digest this news and get into solution mode. "Tell me everything."

"Well, he had some chest pains last week—"

"Last *week*?" I nearly yell.

"Which turned out to be nothing," she quickly adds.

I take a deep breath, trying to dispel the hysteria that surges inside me as she continues.

"But it's put him in kind of a mood since then, and he just seems...I don't know...lethargic, maybe? He didn't want to bother you with it because he knew you'd want to come home, but I felt bad keeping it from you."

Part of me wants to immediately find the cheapest,

quickest flight back to Ohio, even though it will send my credit card balance in the wrong direction.

The rest of me recognizes that this is something I have to face, the consequences of leaving my family behind to follow my own dreams—sacrificing the hours of togetherness for the opportunities here.

I'm touched that they thought they were protecting me, but taking away my choice to be physically present is not something I'm okay with.

Like, what if the worst happened and he didn't make it? Then I would get a random call from Angela or my mom and be completely blindsided.

I shake off that thought because now I'll know to be more on top of my check-ins with my parents and not ignore their calls because it's a slightly inconvenient time for me to answer.

"I'm glad you told me," I say, softening slightly. "But please don't let them keep stuff like this from me. I promise not to make any rash decisions, but I really want to know what's going on."

"Okay," she agrees.

We're both relieved to come to an amicable place on this topic, but I already plan on calling my mom later to get the rundown on all the details.

There's a knock at my door, but before I even have a chance to answer, Will opens it.

"Julianna?" His voice is groggy and a little bit whiny. "Are you awake?"

Angela huffs in my ear. "See? No boundaries. You need to get time and a half—"

"I'll talk to you later," I tell my sister before I hang up

on her, then turn my attention to Will, who is hovering in the doorway. "Everything okay?"

He holds up a note written on a piece of paper with fancy letterhead.

"Mom and Dad went out this morning," Will says. "Can you please help me make food?"

Last time Will tried to make breakfast on his own, he burned his toast so badly that the kitchen smelled like smoke for an entire week.

Not that I'm much better in the kitchen, but I don't hesitate to get up to help him.

"I'm sure we can figure out something," I say.

I try to nudge him toward cereal, but he is adamant about trying to make what he considers a "well-balanced breakfast."

Damn Peter and Amanda and their healthy habits.

A little reluctantly on my part, Will and I decide to try and make omelettes with spinach and other vegetables... only to mess them up so badly that we both just end up with somewhat lumpy scrambled eggs.

We laugh as we try to make our presentation look as good as the plates of food on the recipe site he shows me, but I have to admit, it looks pretty sad.

"It didn't turn out that bad," Will admits after swallowing his first bite.

"Better than dinner last night, at least?"

"No." He shakes his head. "Gabe saved it."

I laugh. "I guess he did."

"Did you know that he is famous?"

"Uh huh."

We eat our breakfasts in silence, exchanging closed-mouth smiles when we meet each other's eyes.

Even from the fourteenth floor, I can hear the occasional siren or honk from below, and I find the noise comforting, like a steady soundtrack to the pulse of the city.

"Pancake is a pretty funny name for a dog," Will says after swallowing another bite.

"Yeah," I agree, wishing we had pancakes to eat right now instead of this.

"Gabe said anytime I want to come along for a walk with her or hang out and play, I can."

I raise my eyebrow. "When did he say this?"

"This morning."

Seeing my confusion, Will slides his phone over to me, open on what appears to be a long conversation.

I swipe my finger up and down, eyeing but not really reading the messages they have sent back and forth.

"You've been texting Gabe?"

"Obviously," he says, though his tone isn't unkind—more like he's a little smug about having a new friend to talk to on the weekends.

I slide his phone back to him. "Wow."

"He even went with my recommendations on how to update his computer system and which new PlayStation to buy. I think we're going to play together online sometimes."

"That's great," I say.

His smile is so wide, it nearly cuts his face in half.

Although I know Angela is right and I should be standing up for the fact that I work nearly twenty-four seven—minus Bagel Fridays and the night I went to Zoe's party—I can't push back about my hours. Because sometimes, it doesn't even feel like work but like I'm taking advantage of the fact that I just get to walk Will to various events and go on errands and keep the house organized.

"I might have also given him your phone number," Will mentions casually with a shrug.

I grin, getting immediate validation at my thoughts that I haven't made a mistake in hanging around this kid so much.

Will stands up and takes his empty plate over to the dishwasher, adding, "I thought you two could also hang out with Pancake and me."

When I get a text from Gabe later that day just to say hello, I have to stop myself from barging into Will's room to give him an appreciative hug.

NINE

Over the next few days, I reluctantly start to agree with Angela.

Maybe it's because she's right about how Amanda and Peter are taking advantage of my situation or maybe it's because I have to spend an entire morning elbows-deep in the oven trying to clean out the smell of salmon and silently lose my cool.

Whatever the reason, I start making changes—they're very slight, but they're there.

Zoe is ecstatic when she discovers I'm now actively trying to have free time, and somehow, she uses this information to convince me to work out.

Angela likes to joke that I'm allergic to exercise, and honestly, part of me thinks she's right.

Gym class was my worst subject in high school. I failed every single practical evaluation but was saved by the written tests on the rules of and information regarding the sports we learned about. Everyone else griped about memorizing the points system in tennis because they just wanted to smash the ball with the racket, but I happily studied.

I hype myself up before I meet Zoe in the lobby, shifting awkwardly in the comfortable athleisure clothes I stole from Angela before I moved.

By the time we leave the building, I'm ready to work up a sweat. At least, that's what I thought the plan was, but it turns out instead of leading me to a running trail or a boxing gym, Zoe and I wind up at a place that looks more like a massage studio than a fitness center.

We spend most of the hour on mats with blankets while a woman walks around with incense sticks and encourages us to "find our inner movement" before guiding us through a few stretches, all of which require us to be on all fours or lying on our backs.

The class ends with some meditation, and the instructor's voice is so soothing I have to fight to stay awake.

"I feel so damn rejuvenated," Zoe says as we walk back toward our building. "Like all of my stress wrinkles have disappeared and my muscles feel good."

"You don't have any wrinkles," I argue. "But I thought the point was to work out, not relax?"

"It's an added bonus."

I level with her. "I just paid thirty dollars to stretch and be whispered at for an hour."

She laughs. "Well, I count it as exercise."

"What part of that, exactly, was exercise?"

Not that I'm complaining, honestly.

"Don't ruin this for me, Julianna," Zoe groans. "It's

how I'm going to justify all the alcohol I'm going to drink later."

"What?" I balk. "It's Tuesday!"

She shrugs. "I'm planning on meeting up with a guy for a drink."

"You're just as bad as my sister. All these weeknight outings with socializing and swiping on dating apps."

"Well, unlike you, I don't have a steady job. One of the perks is that I get to do things like hook up with some guy who thought I looked hot in my little red bikini photos from last summer."

"All credited to these vigorous workouts, right?" I deadpan.

She laughs, and the sound of it echoes in the lobby of our building.

"You tease, but I swear it works," she presses. "And so does my post-workout smoothie, which you are absolutely coming over to try out right now."

I check the time, purely out of habit, and have no reason to argue with her.

She babbles about all the healthy perks to her concoction, telling me that she got the recipe from some celebrity trainer with a television show who worked with Gabe on one of his action movies.

It's a funny contrast to hear her talking about the merits of chia seeds considering she has been inhaling nicotine from her vape pen the entire walk to and from the studio.

Once we're in Gabe's kitchen, I stand by as she pulls a frightening amount of frozen fruit and leafy green vegetables from the freezer.

"Just sit and watch me make magic happen," she insists.

She continues to tout the benefits of all the vitamins as she flips the switch on the blender.

The sound sends Pancake running into her bedroom, but she continues on, watching the ingredients churn into a weird shade of dirt brown.

"Thank you," I say, grateful that it at least looks smooth in the glass.

"Cheers," she calls brightly.

I take a tentative sip, expecting it to taste mostly of grass, but it's actually pretty good.

The frozen blueberries and pineapple cut the earthiness of the vegetables into something palatable, and apparently, the various seeds she used give it a healthy level of plant-based proteins and fats.

I take a picture of it and send it to Angela.

My sister is baffled I have a friend who convinced me to pay to exercise—although she doesn't yet have the details that I didn't even break a sweat—and also got me to attend a party.

"I once did a juice and smoothie cleanse for fourteen days," Zoe tells me as she hops up on the counter, fluttering her bare feet outward like they need a stretch after vigorous activity.

"And you liked it so much that you wanted to keep it up?" I ask.

She frowns and wrinkles her nose. "No, actually, I'm pretty sure it was the worst two weeks of my life."

"When she broke it, she ate an entire pizza," Gabe says, joining us in the kitchen. "Like, a giant, New York style pizza, covered in toppings."

"Yeah, but they were *vegetables*," Zoe defends herself.

Gabe snorts and grabs a drink from the fridge.

I stifle a gasp when he turns to face me full-on.

His hair, which had been a tad overgrown and shaggy, is trimmed, parted, and swept back, somehow making the blue of his eyes stand out even more.

"Whoa," Zoe says, having a completely different reaction than I am. "What happened to you?"

"Final wardrobe fitting ended early," he explains, rubbing a hand over his freshly shaved face.

I force my fingers to grip the cup in front of me, when really, they want to run across his jaw.

Gabe and I have exchanged a few texts since Will kindly shared my phone number with him, and I've learned more about Gabe's plans for the next few months.

He's been managing promotion for a recent film he starred in while wrapping up pre-production on some sort of 1920s romantic drama that's going to be filmed in Queens until the end of January. After that wraps, he's then off to Australia for an action role that's being touted as "the next James Bond," and the cycle of production continues from there.

"Aww, poor Gabriel, did the studio veto your proposal of a more grizzly gangster?" Zoe asks, pinching the edge of his cheek playfully.

"And for that, I'm taking this." He swipes her half-empty smoothie from her hands and drains the rest of it while she whines.

"Just please tell me they don't have women running around in flapper dresses," I say, finally finding my voice.

"I saw a few," Gabe admits. "But not in any of my screen tests."

"What's wrong with flappers?" Zoe asks me.

"Everyone always associates those outfits with that decade, but most of the women didn't actually bother with fringe back then," I explain. "Plus, the fit of most Halloween costumes these days has been modernized to flatter what's popular for our figures, not what was emphasized in that decade."

"Right," Zoe says after a pause. "Your weird history memorization thing."

"It's both a gift and a curse," I admit with a sigh.

Gabe laughs. "Well, I think I'll be okay, especially now that they've forced me to shave and get a haircut, even though I'll be wearing a hat for most of my scenes."

The thought of Gabe wearing a three-piece suit makes me want to break onto the film set and see it for myself.

"We need to see pictures," Zoe insists.

Zoe King is now my favorite person alive.

"Who says I have any?" Gabe deflects.

She glares at him. "I'm willing to bet anything that Rina sent you a batch to choose from for your social feeds."

Gabe smiles, then he shows us both the stills and talks a little bit about what look goes with what scene.

I try my hardest to pay attention, but not having read the script combined with the scent of spearmint and how close I stand to him to look at his phone means I'm just *a little bit* distracted.

"You two should definitely come by the set sometime," Gabe says. "When we officially start filming."

I say, "That sounds awesome," at the same time Zoe says, "Hard pass."

"What?" I ask her. "You don't want to go?"

"In theory, it sounds cool, but in reality, it's a lot of sitting around and waiting. It's kind of like a football game, really. A lot of planning and busywork for, like, thirty seconds at a time of something actually happening." She dramatically sighs and shakes her head. "I dated a quarter-back in college. Even worse decision than the juice cleanse."

"You don't complain when you make the PAs run around to do your bidding," Gabe reminds her.

"Oh, please, they were thrilled at the chance to have an 'in' with the sister of a big star," she says. "Plus, I had to have massive amounts of caffeine for all the monologuing in that one indie film you did last fall."

"Don't let her skew your perspective," Gabe encourages me. "I think you'll like it."

"I think I would, too," I say. "Probably better than yoga and meditation."

"You're hopeless," Zoe says with mock exasperation. "I'm going to go shower and get ready for my date, and you two can plan yours."

She saunters away so innocently, but I don't miss the smirk on her face.

I also silently freak out about her word choice, but it doesn't appear to bother Gabe at all.

Is that what we're doing? Dating?

"So, you told her?" Gabe asks once we're alone.

I swallow down my surprise. "I assumed you did," I admit.

"I didn't get the chance to."

I smile. "She was annoyed that I dropped the news that you and I had plans for this weekend right before we had to settle down for that ridiculous class, so she didn't get to grill me. If anything, one of very few perks of the silent and supposedly soothing practice was that by the end, she seemed to have forgotten about it in favor of all the smoothie talk."

He laughs. "So, we're still on for Saturday?"

"I'm free after I get back from Will's piano lesson."

"How about I pick you up around seven?"

"Oh no," I groan. "You're one of those 'around' people, aren't you?"

His forehead wrinkles in confusion. "What do you mean?"

"Like, for me, if you say seven, I mean seven on the dot," I explain. "But *around* seven can mean fifteen minutes before or after. I just can't live with that type of ambiguity in my life."

"And you shouldn't have to," Gabe insists, barely suppressing a smile. "I will pick you up at exactly seven o'clock."

I like that he's obliging me, but I still frown because I'm not sure how Amanda and Peter would react to that.

Well, to any person showing up to their home at my request—not just because it's *him*.

"How about we meet in the lobby?"

I see a flicker of surprise roll across Gabe's features, like no one has ever been embarrassed to be seen with him before.

"Sure," he agrees. "So, Saturday. Seven. Dinner. A little fancy, but not too fancy. Meeting in the lobby."

"Yes," I say with enthusiasm. "I'm looking forward to it."

When I get back to the Finch apartment, the excitement bubbling up inside me deflates at the expressions on Amanda and Peter's faces.

She looks like she just sucked on a lemon, whereas he lazily scans over my appearance. They sit side by side on the couch that faces the front door; the television is off, and Will is nowhere to be found.

This doesn't exactly seem like a recipe for my success.

"Everything okay?" I ask, gripping my purse like it's going to defend me from whatever they're about to say.

"We wanted to speak with you," Amanda answers tightly and gestures for me to sit.

"Okay," I say slowly, then I take a seat across from them in an uncomfortable but very stylish chair.

Amanda sighs dramatically while Peter looks on, content to stare at me rather than give in to whatever his wife wants to confront me about.

"We have some concerns," she starts, folding her hands on her lap to make herself appear more poised. "About your dedication to Will."

I expect nitpicking over the way I clean or put things away, something along those lines, but there is certainly no rational way they could doubt how much I care about their son.

"What do you mean?" I ask.

"It just seems like you are prioritizing other things rather than spending time with him, which is your job. It's why you live here without paying a dime and get your meals covered."

My temper flares as my mind connects the dots. "Can you give me an example?" I ask dryly.

Amanda gestures at my outfit. "Instead of helping him with his homework this evening, you chose personal activities."

"His homework was completed before I left, and you mentioned that you had dinner taken care of, so I assumed I was able to use my free time how I please." I keep my tone as even and light as I can, not wanting to get into a verbal sparring match with the people who are currently funding my life here in New York.

Amanda sighs. "Well, it's not just that. What about two Saturdays ago?"

I sit up slightly, wanting to show strength and not completely let her bulldoze me. "Amanda, Peter, in the past few months of employment, I've worked nearly every waking hour, so I'm a little confused as to why it's an issue for me to take a few hours to myself when Will is taken care of and you don't have plans."

I deliberately stop myself from bringing up the fact that they're in violation of about a half dozen labor laws—there's a reason why they have to get a new nanny every few months. I can't let this business relationship break down completely until I have myself together and a little more money saved.

Thankfully, Amanda keeps her composure and momentarily directs her annoyance at Peter, who is contributing nothing to this conversation.

"Well then," she says. "The least you can do is give us a few days' notice moving forward."

"Fair enough," I relent. "I'd like to request time off for Saturday night, please."

"Don't we have that event?" Amanda asks Peter.

He sighs and pulls out his phone.

I'm guessing he's flipping to his calendar app to confirm her ability to deny me an evening of happiness.

"No," he answers.

"Are you certain? I thought we had that dinner at Mariana's."

"That's next month."

Amanda huffs as she brings her attention back to me. "Fine."

"Great," I say with a big, fake smile. "Is there anything else?"

"Nope," Amanda says with a clipped tone.

I head off to take a shower, feeling like this conversation was more of a workout than my yoga class with Zoe.

TEN

I should have guessed this place would be fancy, given its proximity to Central Park, but I'm deceived into thinking Gabe and I are dining at a normal restaurant with high-top tables and a sushi bar until I look at the menu in front of me.

The few dollars I spend each week on Bagel Friday feels like an indulgence, but this place is absolutely absurd.

I've had sushi a few times since moving here and enjoyed it, but now, as I'm eyeing a bento box that's more than sixty dollars, I wonder if what I had even counts.

Not to mention the steak costs more than a monthly Metrocard.

"See anything that looks good to you?" Gabe asks, peering at me over his menu.

I nod and scan the prices, trying to pick out the cheapest thing.

It's edamame.

And it's still sixteen dollars.

"What do you like?" I ask him.

"I usually come here with Zoe, and she wants to split the wagyu trio or the sharable sushi. Both are really good."

"I'm game for either, if you are."

I plan on paying for my half of the meal because I don't want to be another one of those people in his life who expects him to pay for everything, and somehow, the thought of splitting something seems less detrimental to my credit card and soul.

The waitress returns with our wine—some deep red that she recommended—and asks if we're ready to order.

"We'll do the Sushi to Share," Gabe says, looking to me for confirmation.

"Sounds good to me," I agree.

The waitress smiles. "I'll go put that in for you. Let me know if you need anything else, Mr. King."

"Mr. King?" I echo once she's gone. "I don't think any waitstaff member has ever called me anything other than, 'Are you done with that?'"

Gabe laughs and swirls the wine in his glass. "Cheers, Miss Jones."

We clink glasses, not breaking eye contact as we each take a sip.

I'm not a big drinker, but I can tell this wine is good—and expensive, judging by the fact that it actually tastes rich, full, and oaky and not like something that's going to give me a headache.

"I can't believe your sister actually prefers Franzia to something like this."

"Yeah, well, she's always been a bit of a weird one," he says.

"All the best people are."

He considers it. "What makes you weird?"

"You already know the answer to this one," I tell him. "I have years of useless facts based on history, geography, and whatever else in my brain."

"I'd argue that's not weird or useless."

"So if I were to randomly tell you…" I pick a snippet of information from my mind. "That there are no snakes in New Zealand, you'd be okay with it?"

"None?" He quirks an eyebrow. "At all?"

I shake my head. "No land snakes, and I don't think they have sea snakes very often, either."

"Well, that's something to keep in mind if I ever get to film a movie there."

"Pancake won't have to get a rattlesnake vaccine," I tell him.

"See?" he says, holding up his hands. "Very helpful."

I laugh. "What makes you weird?"

"Aside from my general life, where complete strangers walk up to me with packs of spearmint gum…" He pauses and takes a breath. "Probably—"

"Gabe?"

Both our gazes snap toward the voice.

"Melanie," Gabe says, jumping up to offer her a hug. "I thought you were staying in L.A. for the rest of the month?"

"I was planning on it, but Josh convinced Ruby and me to visit for...oh, who's this?" Her gaze meets mine.

I offer her a smile, but she doesn't return it.

Instead, she stands up straighter, like she needs to

protect herself in the presence of someone she doesn't know.

It's the same tick I see in Gabe, the one where he feels he needs to keep his defenses raised around people who might try to take advantage of him.

It kills me knowing they both have probably learned their lessons the hard way.

"Melanie Sonte, this is Julianna Jones," Gabe introduces us.

She extends her hand, and I stand to shake it, feeling her trepidation over not knowing who I am.

"I'm a friend of Zoe's," I say, filling in the blanks for her. "And Gabe's neighbor."

She doesn't soften at all. "Nice to meet you," she responds coolly.

I get the impression that Gabe is not the kind of guy who goes out on a lot of dates—although I haven't allowed myself to seek out that information online or found time to ask him about it personally—so it's a little off-putting that she doesn't warm to the idea of me at all.

"Where's Ruby?" Gabe asks her.

"Waiting in the car." Melanie points over her shoulder with the hand that isn't holding a large bag of takeout. "I came in to pick up our dinner, then saw you over here."

"You'll have to tell her I said hi."

Melanie nods. "You should come by Josh's later."

She says it in a way that makes it clear I'm not invited, and I try not to be too offended by that.

"I think we'll pass tonight," Gabe says. "We have our own plans, and I don't think Josh has recovered from meeting Julianna the first time."

I grimace. "I would have kept my mouth shut if he hadn't pushed me, but you know how passionate I am about historical accuracy..."

"*Weirdly* passionate," Gabe says with a wink.

"But not useless, apparently," I respond.

Melanie's eyes flash in my direction, like she's seeing me as a totally different person. "You're the one Josh was telling me about."

I don't know if that's a good thing or a bad thing.

Gabe nods and gestures back to our table. "Well, we're going to get back to it, but I'll text you tomorrow to see if you want to grab coffee."

"I'd like that," she says, giving me a final appraising glance before she heads out.

Our dinner arrives just as Gabe and I settle back in. The waitress sticks around long enough to remind us what each roll is—although I lose track after the fifth kind—then we're on our own, fumbling with chopsticks.

"Is this the snow crab one?" Gabe asks, picking up one of the many pieces to inspect it more closely.

"I thought you'd eaten this before?"

"Eating with Zoe means I have to inhale food if I want any for myself, and I don't get time to appreciate or even really figure out what I'm enjoying."

"My sister's like that, too," I say with a laugh, recalling how many times our mom had to step in and play referee to split up our dinner.

"Tell me about her," Gabe prompts.

"Where do I start?" I say, then dive right in.

We actually end up spending the entirety of the meal talking about our families.

My life in Ohio actually seems pretty similar to his upbringing in Connecticut—well, right up until his life blew up when he got cast as Eggy Smith.

Even then, his parents tried to keep him grounded, sending him to his normal public school when they weren't shooting.

By all accounts, we had somewhat equal lives up to a point, so it's interesting to think of how different our situations are currently. Gabe's a gorgeous, wealthy, and put-together man who has the world at his fingertips and is already so accomplished in his career. And I'm just...one of the millions of people who are trying to figure out how to chase what they really want in life.

I argue with Gabe over paying, but the waitress swoops in to let me know the meal has already been taken care of as a show of gratitude—meaning neither of us even has to pick up the check. Although, I do see him drop a sizable cash tip on the table before he leads me out the back entrance to a car waiting for us.

I'm disappointed by this action, not just because it feels a little strange and sneaky but because I'm not ready for the night to end.

"What do you think about going for a walk?" I suggest before we reach the car.

"A walk sounds nice," he says, then motions for the driver to roll down the window so he can tell him about our change of plans.

The night air is pleasant for October, but the wind is a little cold, cutting through the fabric of my coat like it's nonexistent.

I tighten my bright red scarf, which I think was Angela's at one point, as we walk along the edge of Central Park.

"Do you do this often?" I ask him.

"Date?" Gabe clarifies.

My heart flutters at the confirmation that he and I are actually on a *date* together.

I can't help but smile. "Not what I meant, but now that you've brought it up..."

He laughs and shoves his hands in his pockets. "It's been a while," he admits. "I've had girlfriends here and there, but they always end the same way."

"What does that mean?" I ask tentatively.

"That my schedule is exhausting," he says with a grimace. "And for a long time, I put my career before everything else."

"But that's no longer the case?" I clarify.

He's contemplative for a few steps before he answers. "I was really, truly lucky to be Eggy, and I've never shied away from that because I have so many loyal fans who have supported my career through the years...but eventually, I thought I had something to prove."

"To who?"

Gabe shakes his head. "Everyone, I guess. I was so determined to be seen as a serious actor that I took on a bunch of projects I wasn't passionate about just to test myself. And then I started getting typecast, and to break out of it, I basically sold my soul to a studio for a three-picture deal. But this is the last one I'm under contract for."

I have no idea how this stuff works, but I'm more interested in Gabe's mindset than the logistics of the contracts at the moment. "And then what?"

He smiles, keeping his gaze ahead like he's momentarily lost in thought. "One of the last things my mom said to me before she died was, 'Just remember, Gabriel, life isn't a big rehearsal for something. This is your life, and you shouldn't waste it being unhappy.'"

"That should be on a poster somewhere," I say dreamily. "'This is your life.'"

"It is a good reminder, and it's one that I'm going to keep in mind as I move forward. I don't need to prove anything to anyone...I just want to do what feels right."

I nod. "It sounds like a great way to honor your mother's memory. And to live your life."

"Thank you, Miss Jones," he says, attempting to lighten the conversation.

"But I do have one more question," I jump in before he can swap topics completely.

"Hit me with it."

I chew on my bottom lip. "What about you and Melanie? Did you ever..."

"Ah," he says. "Always just friends. *Only* ever friends, despite what everyone seems to think."

"I didn't get the impression that she liked me very much," I admit. "I'm not offended by it. I guess I just read into it incorrectly as to why."

"Melanie is, generally, really guarded with people that she doesn't know," he explains. "For all the rumors and stuff that's happened to me over the years...it's been ten times worse for her. She's scrutinized for things I didn't even know people cared about, like having chipped nail polish or not smiling enough during interviews or wearing something that's the wrong color."

I frown. "I didn't consider that."

"She'll warm up to you eventually," Gabe says. "It'll just take time."

I like that he's suggesting that there will be longevity to whatever it is we're doing. "Okay."

"When was your last relationship?" Gabe asks, continuing our volley of questions back and forth.

"First year of grad school," I tell him automatically.

"What happened?"

"Nothing big or dramatic. It's not really that different from what you described with your past relationships. I think sometimes people just aren't the right fit for each other, and it's easy to walk away. Which is probably easier for me because I don't have millions of people trying to dig into my personal life all the time."

Gabe smiles. "I do get some anonymity just by living in such a big city, but I don't really hang out in many places outside of our little neighborhood."

"I was wondering why you wanted to live in an area kind of disconnected from the city instead of, like, the Village or something more popular for people under age fifty," I joke.

"Don't knock the older crowd," Gabe says. "Some of my most devoted fans are Boomers with a very serious Eggy fascination."

I giggle and shake my head as he takes out a pack of spearmint gum and accept a piece when he offers it.

We continue our walk while we chew, him cracking the gum between his molars.

"Will you tell me more about the thing with you and facts?" Gabe asks. "When did it start?"

"I don't even know when it became a thing, to be honest. I've always been interested in the stories behind the story, and I think growing up in an age when Wikipedia was readily accessible enabled me. I like to watch documentaries and read books, but even if it's fiction, I like to find the truth in it and understand more about it."

"That makes sense, then, why you pick up random facts about whatever you stumble across."

"Yeah," I continue. "And I don't even really like classical music, but I once heard a piece of a Beethoven symphony in a commercial, and now I have all this random information about his life in my brain that I don't know what to do with. I went down a rabbit hole about his life and his work, which led me to the branches of information about the German city he grew up in, then the fact that there's a crater on Mercury named after him, and...it's really endless how much sticks with me."

"You're basically a case study of why parents shouldn't allow their kids to use the internet unsupervised."

I laugh. "Tell that to the Beethoven historian I emailed back and forth with for a few months. He even sent me a signed copy of one of his books."

"Now *that* is pretty impressive."

"You say impressive; I say psychotic."

He chuckles as we wait for the crosswalk signal to turn, then continue to wind through all the blocks that will lead us home.

"You never got the chance to tell me what's weird about you," I remind him.

"I really like to garden. I spent an entire summer break in my teens helping my mom redo the backyard, and I loved every single second of figuring out where to plant everything, what kind of fertilizer to use, all of it."

"That's not weird, Gabe. That's actually very sweet."

He rubs the back of his neck while trying to come up with another answer. "Well, how about the fact that my favorite way to watch television is on mute with subtitles?"

I roll my eyes in response. "That seems like a weird actor thing."

"I use Q-tips obsessively, even though every doctor ever says you're not supposed to use them on the insides of your ears."

"Nice try."

"I love the smell of gasoline."

"Next."

"After taking girls out for a first date of sushi, we take a long walk home, and I murder them before we reach the lobby."

I can't help but laugh at that one. "Just give up," I say. "You're just a normal guy, Gabe King. Nothing you can say will change my mind on that."

"Yeah," he says, like he's allowing himself to believe the words I say. "Maybe I am."

ELEVEN

I answer my phone without even seeing who is calling because it's definitely too early for me to open my eyes, let alone expose them to the harsh light.

I immediately regret the decision, though, because Angela's voice shrieks in my ear.

Her shrillness causes me to bolt upright, assuming that something awful has happened at home.

My brain is slow to process her rapid fire words, but once it does, I groan and sink back against the pillows.

"HOW COULD YOU NOT TELL ME ABOUT THIS?" Angela continues on. "I THOUGHT IT WAS WEIRD THAT YOU DIDN'T SEND ME ANY PICTURES YESTERDAY, BUT I JUST ASSUMED YOU WERE INSIDE DOING NOTHING LIKE YOU ARE ALWAYS DOING."

"Angela," I try to interrupt, but she keeps going.

"I CANNOT BELIEVE MY OWN SISTER WAS KEEPING THIS FROM ME!"

"Stop yelling at me, or I'm going to hang up the phone."

"FINE!"

Her words falter, but I can hear how heavy her breathing is from being so worked up.

Angela groans. "I can't believe you let me go on and on about a freaking *handshake* when you've been living this totally secret life."

"What are you talking about?" I ask her.

"CHECK YOUR MESSAGES!"

"Okay, okay, just lower the volume."

As I pull my phone away from my ear, I can still hear her ranting at me, even though I haven't put my phone on speaker.

On my screen, I see missed texts from Gabe, in which he apologizes profusely, and then a bunch of links and pictures from Angela.

Apparently, a photographer followed Gabe and me home last night.

The shots aren't that great—Gabe is defined and caught in the streetlights in some of them, while I remain almost a complete blur.

In fact, I don't think anyone outside my immediate family would recognize the shape of my face from the angle or distance.

I bring the phone back to my ear. "And you're certain this is me?" I question, biting back a smile.

"Don't give me that," she snaps. "You're wearing my scarf. You know, the one our *very dead* grandmother hand-knitted for me during our last Christmas together."

"Don't act like you're upset. You didn't even get along with Granny."

"Anyway, when I went back and looked at Gabe King's

feed and saw the photo of the woman he's supposedly dating, you know, the picture with the legs? Imagine my surprise at seeing that nasty scar on your shin—"

"Nasty?" I interrupt, tossing back the covers to inspect the jagged line for myself.

"And I knew that your friend Zoe looked familiar," she presses on. "I just can't believe you kept this from me! I'm supposed to be your sister. Your best friend. Your confidant in all things hot celebrity secret boyfriends!"

I roll my eyes at her dramatics. "Did Mom and Dad see this?"

"What the hell would Mom and Dad be doing on a gossip site at six in the morning?" Angela asks incredulously.

I would like to know what *anyone*, especially my sister, is doing on a gossip site at six in the morning, but I don't ask.

"Angela," I sigh into the phone.

"Don't *breathe* at me, you little secret hoarder," Angela seethes. "How long has this been going on? What is even going on? Who are you? Am I going to be invited to all sorts of fancy Hollywood parties now? Are you going to be on the cover of magazines and stuff?"

"I'm going to hang up on you if you don't calm down."

She huffs. "Cut me some slack, Jules. How would you feel if you just casually stumbled across the news that I was dating someone, let alone someone who is practically American royalty?"

I don't like her play on words, but I can understand her point.

"I was going to tell you eventually," I say. "But honestly, there's not much to update you on yet."

"Tell me every little thing. Right now." She takes a breath. "Please."

I burrow down under the covers, and once I'm settled, I proceed to catch her up from the very beginning.

She needs a minute to look back at the photos I sent weeks ago to confirm that he was in the background of them—because apparently my explanation wasn't enough to get her to believe me—then she grows a little bit smug and takes some of the credit for us meeting in the first place.

I haven't studied chaos theory or the butterfly effect in depth, but even if Gabe and I hadn't bumped into each other, I think I still would have met Zoe and Pancake in the elevator…and then he and I would have met eventually.

Maybe?

But if that happened, would we have had such sparks had I not felt so off-kilter by his anger and him being so vehemently against my existence?

That's probably not the recommended way to begin a relationship, but I felt drawn to him from the very beginning in a way I didn't quite understand.

I haven't been able to purge him from of my mind since, even back when he seemed to not like me very much.

"And so you just parted ways at the elevator last night, no hug or anything?" Angela asks, bringing me back into our conversation.

I'm pretty sure she has peppered me with more questions in twenty minutes than either Gabe or I have asked each other in the time since we've met.

"What should I have done?" I chuckle. "Offered him a *handshake?*"

I can practically feel Angela's attempt to glare at me from Ohio.

"Oh, shut up," she says, but even she can't hold in her laughter. "You could have pounced on him or something."

"Yeah, that definitely sounds like something I would do," I deadpan.

"Well, you can do it next time," she says brightly. "You are seeing him again, right?"

"I think so. Even though all his texts I caught just now were apologizing for the photos leaking."

Angela squeals. "Hang up on me!"

"What?" I balk.

"Hang up. Right now. Plan a second date. And then jump on him and give me every damn detail."

I only take the first part of her advice, choosing to hang up so I can process this information on my own.

I give myself a few minutes to scroll through all of the speculation about whether the woman with the red scarf is the same mystery woman with the legs from his social media feed before I close them all.

Even though Gabe thinks my trait of rabbit hole research is endearing, I don't think it's healthy for me to read through all the comments and posts for this type of stuff.

I shoot him a text to let him know I appreciate his apology, but it's not worth the headache of getting upset since my identity wasn't revealed...even though I think it's only a matter of time. The Commoners are ruthless sleuths, and I'm sure Rina is fielding a ton of calls and emails from gossip magazines.

If we continue on with whatever we're doing, we'll need

to sit down and have a conversation about what it all means, but for now, I'm happy to enjoy the present of spending time with him and remaining anonymous in the public eye.

My phone buzzes with a text, and I get all excited, hoping it's Gabe, but I frown when I see it's actually from an unknown number.

Is this Julianna Jones?

As soon as I read my name, my heart sinks into my stomach.

All that anonymity I'm grateful for is now out the window. Someone has discovered it is me, has found all of my personal information, and is about to exploit it—after all, my research has taught me that no matter how hard you try to hide information, public records are easy enough to come across.

This is Josh Ortega, Gabe's friend. We met at the party a few weeks ago.

I audibly sigh in relief that my assumption was incorrect and shoot back a message. *Hi. Yeah, it's Julianna.*

Is it okay if I call you right now? I know it's early.

Sure.

Okay.

"Hello?" I answer on the first ring.

"I bet you never thought you'd hear from me again," Josh says lightly, immediately breaking the ice.

"I'm, uh, a little surprised," I admit.

The sounds of wherever he's at in the city come through the phone, so he has to speak up into the receiver.

My preferred morning is to not have two people yell at

me in my ear before I've had breakfast, but it seems I don't have a choice in the matter.

"I'm almost on set," he says. "But I wanted to talk to you about a job."

"A job?" I sputter.

"Some research work for a film I'm working on."

My hands shake in excitement. "Oh?"

"We're doing some preliminary designs, and I need assistance on a few things for some scenes that we're going to film. It's a white collar crime film set in 1970s Chicago. I know it's not your particular area of expertise, but Gabe said that you might be a fit for it."

I swallow.

While nannying doesn't suit my degree and knacks for facts, this definitely would.

It's the first real chance I have at work related somewhat to my field, actually getting paid to do research, and it's crazy to think it's coming from someone I insulted at a party.

"Are you interested?" Josh asks, trying to discern why I'm being so quiet.

I nod enthusiastically at his words only to remember that he can't see it.

"Yes," I say, trying to keep my cool as best I can. "Definitely interested."

"Good." He sighs in relief. "Just text me your email address, and I'll get everything over to you. Details, pay information, an NDA for you to sign, and whatnot. Then you can let me know what you think."

"Okay," I say, a little stunned.

It feels like ever since I met Gabe, I have days that are

complete whirlwinds—today is definitely one of them, and I haven't even fully woken up yet.

Someone, wherever he is, calls for him loud enough that I can hear it on my end.

"All right, I have to go. Talk to you later."

"Wait," I say quickly. "One last thing..."

"Yeah?"

"Did Gabe...pressure you to do this or something? Because as great as this sounds, I don't want to get work based on favors or something like that."

He chuckles. "As much as I sparingly value Gabe's opinion on my line of work, I can confidently say he has absolutely nothing to do with this other than filling me in on your background after I asked. Do you know how hard it is to find good people?"

I don't, really.

"Well, I suppose you don't," he speculates. "But let me tell you, it's really unbelievably hard. Most people treat research and most of the other behind-the-scenes jobs as a way to get in front of the camera or meet famous people, but you actually prefer this kind of stuff, do you not?"

"You're right."

"Okay, I have to go. I'll email you in a bit."

"Okay," I say, but he's already gone.

I drop the phone on my chest and spend the next hour staring at the ceiling and wondering what the hell is happening to my life.

Eventually, Will disturbs my contemplation when he knocks and asks if we can make another round of omelettes.

After I shower and dress, Will and I successfully make a round of eggs.

Peter and Amanda definitely pick up on my good mood as Will and I happily chat, deciding that in the future maybe we could be a little more bold in the kitchen, then we start looking up recipes that we could try out next weekend that don't have any ingredients he's allergic to.

As we join his parents at the table and tuck in, Amanda interrupts our conversation on the complexities of making a quiche.

"How was your evening, Julianna?" she asks, digging her spoon into half a grapefruit.

I don't miss the underlying irritation in her tone.

I momentarily panic, thinking she saw the articles and put together who I was with, something I'm honestly not sure how she'll react to, but after a blink, I realize it's just because she's annoyed I had a night out and she didn't.

"It was fine, thank you," I say, then take an overly large bite of my omelette, buying myself some time to avoid any other prying.

She smiles, and it seems disingenuous. "Did you do anything fun?"

I nod and shovel another bite into my mouth.

She eyes me while I chew thoroughly.

It seems like she's not going to let up until I give her details, and I'm going to make myself sick if I keep shoving food down to avoid speaking.

"A friend and I went out for sushi, then took a walk," I say after swallowing.

Amanda looks at me expectantly, as if there's something else I should have been doing to occupy my time.

"And then I came back here," I add.

"Oh," she says, pleased that I didn't have an evening that was more exciting than hers.

"What's the difference between a quiche and a frittata?" Will asks, still scrolling on his phone.

"I actually don't know," I admit. "How about you look it up and tell us?"

For the remainder of breakfast, I try to solely focus on Will's questions and my food, but eventually, I lose my appetite under Amanda's glare and spend the rest of the day hiding in Will's room while he plays video games and I try to concentrate on reading a book.

TWELVE

I don't see Gabe for three weeks.

It's a little frightening how I already feel a noticeable void without his presence, but I do my best to stay busy and not obsess over how scary that is.

Aside from my normal nannying and Bagel Friday duties, I start and complete the research Josh asked me to do a full two months before the deadline. Josh was baffled when I let him know that, but he set up time for us to meet in person to review my work.

It was an interesting challenge and one that required a serious binge of academic texts, documentaries, and looking at hundreds of photos, but the hours I poured into it should pay off into the kind of accuracy I need to see on screen.

When we sit down at a table at a coffee shop near Union Square on the agreed upon day, I can tell he's equal parts curious and skeptical of what I've put together.

But as I begin to walk him through the report, I watch his demeanor shift.

He's still a little direct and standoffish—but that might just be his personality—but he seems to be nothing short of impressed.

It also helps that he tells me so repeatedly.

Somewhat luckily, I've been aware of the intricacies in dialogue and fashion of the area and era in the Windy City because last spring, I got a little obsessed with the Sears Tower for about six hours—and that was long enough to ingest a ton of information.

The completion of the building happened in 1973, and there are a surprising number of videos online detailing fashion and culture in that era, giving me the ability to fact-check my suggestions against multiple outlets and resources.

The last thing I want to do is overwhelm him or whoever needs to translate this information into a script or film with details, so I put a few notes corresponding with what's in the script, then flagged where to find more information in the massive index with reference articles, photos, and screenshots that I compiled.

Truly, I should have asked for clarification on the entirety of the process and what falls under his jurisdiction as set design, but once I go down a rabbit hole, it's tough to climb out of it.

"This is...wow," Josh says, flipping through a few pages.

It's a ringing endorsement, appeasing my ego enough to let me relax, sit back, and watch him take in everything.

"You know, most people just annotate the script and

email it over to me," Josh says in the lightest tone I've heard yet.

I frown. "I guess I'm not most people."

He shakes his head like he's trying to expel that negativity from my mind before it takes root. "And that's a good thing. Trust me."

It's not like I have another option.

He pulls out his phone, which is lighting up with a reminder notification. "I actually have to run out to my next meeting, but this is really great work, Julianna," he compliments. "I'm tied up for the next few months, but would you want to do this again in the future?"

"That would be great." I try not to come across as too excited, but I'm fidgeting under the table.

Not only is this a fantastic resume-builder, but I actually enjoyed the work.

"I also have some industry friends who might be interested in some research help," Josh says, not even looking up from his screen while he talks. "I have one friend who is pulling her hair out over some dystopian television series. Anyway, I'll put the word out and catch you later."

"Thank you so much," I gush.

He smiles at me and shakes my hand before he goes outside to hail a cab.

I take a minute for myself, processing the opportunity that landed in my lap, and excitedly text Gabe the news.

As I walk back to the Finch apartment, I try not to dwell on the fact that my messages have gone unreturned.

Gabe hasn't been the best at responding since I last saw him because he's usually on set without his phone, but he tries to compensate for it when he is available, sending me long updates about the project and telling me he misses me.

I check my phone for the tenth time as I enter the lobby, then I finally break down and check the internet for leaked photos and movie updates.

Unfortunately for me, most of the coverage is from a scene where he has to passionately kiss his co-star, and then there are a few pictures of Melanie visiting the set, sending Eggy fans into wild speculation about them being together.

As I'm pulling at the ends of my hair in frustration, the elevator doors open to reveal Zoe and Pancake, and although I don't blab a word of what I'm thinking, she picks up on my mood.

She then insists on taking Gabe up on his offer for me to visit him on set, even though she told both of us weeks ago that she'd basically rather die than do that.

And now, days later, after finally groveling long enough to Amanda to get a full day off for Gabe's birthday—although she doesn't know that information—I'm second-guessing that decision completely.

"Just stick close to me," Zoe says reassuringly.

I don't know if she's picking up on my nervousness, but I'm tempted to ask her if I can have a hit from her vape, even though my lungs would rebel against the action.

The security guard at the front of the lot returns our IDs and slides badges through the window, instructing us to wear them at all times unless we want to be escorted off the premises.

"Thanks again for doing this," I tell her as we walk toward the massive white building.

It looks like a warehouse, so it's fitting that our path is lined with trailers and construction equipment.

"Of course," she says. "It's not like I have anything else going on anyway."

That makes me frown.

Zoe is normally all confidence and smiles, but occasionally she'll mutter some comment about what she calls her "non-existent and joke of a career."

She's kind of like Gabe that way, putting on a show for other people.

Or maybe we all do that—hiding our true selves from the world in fear of social stigma or rejection or vulnerability.

I don't have a chance to argue with her choice of working because Gabe rushes toward us.

He's all smiles in his full 1920s costume, a three-piece suit and his hair slicked back with an off-center part.

My jaw drops open at how unbelievable he looks.

"Don't drool all over yourself," Zoe murmurs with a laugh.

I close my mouth. "Sorry."

"For what?" Gabe asks, finally reaching us.

Zoe waves him off. "Nothing, birthday boy. How much longer until you're needed?"

"They just called for me," he says with a tight smile. "But we can catch up at lunch?"

I nod and offer him a shy smile before he pulls me in for a quick hug that's all spearmint and wool.

"Happy birthday," I tell him through the rush of warmth I feel at his arms around me.

"I'm so glad you're here," he murmurs before we part,

and then he's rushed off by a woman wearing a headset and a stern look.

"Let's go watch and force someone to get us coffee," Zoe says, holding out her arm for me to loop mine through.

I laugh. "Sounds good to me."

Zoe, apparently, knows everyone on the crew.

She gives out hugs and introductions with nearly every step we take on our brief tour until we're perched on director chairs in front of a set of monitors where we can see the speakeasy setup in all its glory.

On film, it'll be a roaring affair, but in person, the extras are all silent, acting like they're carrying on conversations by moving their mouths but without actually making any sound.

I can see it from my vantage point easily enough, even though there are a few dozen crew members and modern day electronics setups, but I watch the screens because they give me an up close and personal look at Gabe.

There's an incredible amount of coordination that happens between each take, with slight adjustments to lighting and touch-ups on makeup. This director is a fanatic for detail, requesting that some of the extras even have glasses topped off or make costume changes.

Even though it's going to be probably a three-minute scene in the movie, Gabe has to repeat his lines at least twelve times before we break for lunch.

He joins us, careful not to spill anything on his suit while the three of us chat about the differences of this film compared to others, and Gabe informs us that he is particularly excited to get out of this soundstage to film some shots on location next week.

When things resume after lunch, the cameras are in slightly different positions, even though all the motions and lines are the same.

I'm more than content to watch, but Zoe seems completely bored while she lazily scrolls on her phone.

I'm caught up in the movie magic so completely that I'm jarred when the crew wheels out a massive cake that's covered in twenty-seven candles, announcing Gabe's birthday and that filming is wrapped for the day.

Most of the cast members don't partake in the dessert, complaining about sugar and macros and things like that, but Zoe and I happily dig into our slices alongside some crew members.

"Why don't you take a slice over to Gabe's trailer?" Zoe suggests, shoving another plate into my hands.

"Is that okay?" I ask.

She nods and nudges me away with her elbow to the trailer she, thankfully, pointed out earlier.

I tentatively cross the lot, feeling like I shouldn't be allowed to walk around on my own, but I muster up my courage as I juggle both plates in one hand so I can knock on the door.

"Come in," he calls after shuffling around for a beat.

I pull the latch on the door in time to see him slide on a plain shirt. Not wanting a repeat of my earlier gawking, I avert my eyes.

"I'm decent," he says playfully.

I meet his gaze and hold out the plate of cake for him. "I wasn't sure if you got a piece."

He accepts the plate with a grin. "Just don't tell my nutritionist."

"Things are that strict, even for this movie?" I ask him, surprised.

He shakes his head. "I've already started training for one early next year in Australia. It's a grueling program, and it'll be worth it, but I'm already sick of grilled chicken."

We take a seat on the little couch at the end of the trailer, and I'm close enough to see his suppressed elation at the taste of frosting and once again inhale the scent of him.

"I got you something," I say after a few beats, rifling through my purse with one hand.

"You didn't have to do that."

I chuckle. "Why do people always do that?"

He sets his empty plate down on the counter and turns back toward me. "Do what?"

"Tell a person they didn't have to buy them a gift," I say. "I know I didn't, but I wanted to. Plus, it's just a little thing."

"And now you should let me say that people tend to diminish the meaning of their gifts by saying 'it's just a little thing' when it's actually a nice gesture."

"Point taken," I concede. "We both can improve. Now, hold out your hands."

I don't miss the flash of excitement that overtakes his features, and I just hope the more time we spend together, the less guarded he becomes.

"Are you going to make me close my eyes?" Gabe teases.

"No," I say, then pull my hand out of my bag and deposit a little pack of gum onto his waiting palms.

At first, he's confused, then after a blink, he smiles before breaking out into loud laughter.

I agonized over whether to get something at all, but when Amanda sent me to the pharmacy yesterday for one of Will's many prescriptions, I stood at the counter long enough to impulse buy a pack of Big Red.

"I thought it might be time for a new flavor," I tell him. "As much as I like spearmint, I thought that, given your new lease on life, you might want to change things up."

"It's perfect," he says, holding the package between his thumb and forefinger.

When he looks at me again, his expression is utterly serious.

"*You* are perfect, Julianna."

"Oh, I don't know about—"

He cuts off my argument by capturing my lips in his.

My forgotten plate falls to the floor as I reach for him, unbothered by anything in this world that isn't him or what is happening with us.

He tastes all sugary from the icing, but it's a little deceptive because his actions are anything but sweet—they're deliberate, raw, and a little rough as he slides his hands into my hair.

I gasp when he pulls me closer and deepens the kiss, tongue sliding along my lip.

I'm being absolutely owned by Gabe King's mouth, and it's the hottest thing to ever happen to me.

I start to shake with adrenaline or anticipation or who knows what. I reach out and grab a hold of his chest to steady myself, but it doesn't stop my entire body from trembling.

Without breaking apart, I climb onto his lap, craving just a little more friction between us.

"Yes," I whisper as his hands travel down my spine.

He smiles. "Yes," he confirms, then captures my lips once again.

I ache to be under his touch and explored by him, but I'm also content to draw this out as long as possible because each second feels better than the last, like we're slowly learning and building and working toward something truly spectacular.

Every doubt and minute of second-guessing I had while we were apart fades away as his hands press into my lower back, just above my ass, to grind my hips down onto him.

A low moan claws out from the back of my throat, and I'm aware of his grin before I lose all sense of myself to the rhythm between us.

I should be embarrassed by how turned on I am, but it's been a long time since I've been touched like this.

And honestly, I don't think any man has ever made me feel this much so quickly.

I'm melting, and we're only *kissing*.

It takes everything in me to not surrender to him completely at this moment, but I let myself enjoy the feeling between us, and more importantly, enjoy him.

We continue tasting each other, flying high above everything else in the world, until Zoe makes a big production of knocking on the door and calling for us to come back to reality.

"Gabriel," she calls in a singsong voice.

The lust cloud we've been enveloped in dissipates, halting our movement as we reluctantly break our kiss.

I open my eyes and am extraordinarily pleased to find we're both red-faced and panting heavily—because it's clear that I have just as much of an effect on him as he does on me.

“I’ve wanted to do that for a while,” he admits quietly between breaths, catching the ends of my hair in his fingertips.

I nod, not ready to try my voice just yet, and plant another soft kiss on his lips before I stand.

I expect Gabe to join me, but he shifts on the couch, leaning forward to rest his elbows on his knees.

“I, uh, need a minute,” he says, letting his smile tug at the side of his mouth.

“You do?” I ask, then the realization dawns on me, and I try to suppress the giggles. “Oh. You do.”

“Come on, guys, I’m bored,” Zoe whines from the other side of the door. “I’m coming in if you’re not coming out.”

“I’ll go,” I tell him. “You stay here and…yeah.”

He drops his head and closes his eyes, letting out a sigh that I feel so deeply, I immediately wonder when I can have him to myself again.

THIRTEEN

Over the next few weeks, I visit the set two more times on my own, allowing myself to be fully immersed in the experience instead of listening to Zoe's snide comments and swear words.

Gabe and I barely get time alone to continue what we started in his trailer, but he does manage to carve out a window to accompany me on one Bagel Friday outing.

He doesn't indulge in a blueberry bagel, though, simply going for a large cup of coffee and listening to a sleep-deprived Carl update me on Mary and their new baby boy.

Finally, after what feels like years of torture, Gabe and I both get time off on the same night.

I don't know about Gabe, but I hope to take full advantage of it.

It would definitely be too forward of me to suggest we just stay in his apartment, but it doesn't mean I don't want to.

I'm practically starving for his touch, and the thought of him and me alone, with a bed in close proximity, is what fills my mind as I wait for Will to finish up his piano lesson.

Gabe has been texting me all week, telling me he has a surprise in mind, which has me curious and slightly on edge

I'm not the biggest fan of being kept out of the loop, so aside from my less than appropriate thoughts, my mind runs wild with speculation about what his plans are.

He refused to budge on details, but he did mention that casual clothes were totally fine, so at the very least, I know I won't show up to some sort of black-tie event in my favorite pair of black jeans.

But I do take the time to do all the necessary grooming and slide on my matching black lace thong and bra set—the only pieces I own that might actually qualify as lingerie.

I finish getting ready right before I'm supposed to meet Gabe in the lobby, and my attempt to leave the Finch apartment unnoticed seems almost possible until my hand is *just* out of reach of the doorknob.

"Going somewhere?" Peter asks from his spot on the couch.

The sound of his voice makes me jump out of my skin, but I have to remind myself that I requested the evening off well in advance, and I'm not doing anything wrong.

I hate how this job and living situation have made me second-guess enjoying my own time.

"I have the night off," I remind him as I tug my jacket on.

He drops the newspaper he was reading, like some sort of supervillain, and gazes at me. "Where are you off to?"

"None of your business" is what I want to tell him, but instead, I say, "Out with a friend."

"Which friend?"

At this, I turn back to finally look at him.

There's a darkness to his expression, eyes narrowed and lips pulled tight into a line.

Angela likes to say I have an added sense about people, discerning every bit of a person's body language and silence cues to read into what they're thinking.

It's probably true, but I think anyone looking at Peter in this moment would see how he thinks he has some control over my comings and goings—and that he might even get off on it a little bit.

The show of power is usually subtle, but I don't stick around to see if it's going to be more defined.

"Have a good night, Peter," I say before I let myself out.

I dash toward the elevator, and part of me expects him to follow, playing out some sick and twisted worst case scenario in my mind.

Once I'm in the safety of the elevator, I exhale and pull my jacket tighter around me. The feel of the fabric and the warmth help me collect myself.

Peter clearly wanted to get under my skin, and I refuse to let him be a silent, overbearing presence on my date with Gabe, so I mentally try to shake off the encounter and fix a smile on my face.

I falter just a bit when I find Gabe's not in the lobby waiting for me to arrive, but as I reach for my phone to check the time, the concierge approaches to tell me that Gabe's already out front.

I thank him as he appreciatively eyes the silver Lamborghini outside the doors, but I'm only interested in the man sitting on the hood.

"Hey," Gabe says, pushing off his perch.

If I owned something this expensive, I wouldn't take it out of the garage, let alone use it as a bench while I wait for a date.

It's another level of being rich I can't relate to, much like people who don't put cases on their iPhones—I'm brave in many ways but not that one.

"Nice car," I tell him as he opens the passenger door for me.

"Thanks," Gabe returns lightly, then closes my door and dashes around to the driver's side. "It's my one vice."

I give him a challenging look. "What about spearmint gum?"

"Didn't you hear?" He settles in and turns the ignition. "I'm more of a cinnamon guy now."

I chuckle at that, relieved that my lingering unease from my interaction with Peter evaporates in Gabe's presence. "You know, my dad once told me that you can't trust anyone without a vice."

"Wise words."

"Oh please," I huff. "Your mom gives you fantastic life advice and words to live by, whereas I just get the urge to enable people's bad habits."

He smiles, then double-checks to make sure we're in the clear before he pulls out and accelerates toward downtown. This choice of direction means I'm able to cross off

Central Park, the Upper West Side, Harlem, and the Bronx from my list of where we could possibly be heading this evening.

"Are you going to tell me what you have planned?" I ask.

"Where's the fun in that?"

"It's fun for you, maybe. Nerve-racking for me."

Gabe reaches for my hand, threading his fingers with mine.

There's something comforting yet sexy about how big and warm his palms are, and I can only imagine what it would feel like to have those running along my bare skin all the way down to my—

"Don't you trust me?" Gabe asks, tone teasing.

I blink and force myself to focus on our banter, not all the things I want him to do to me. "Of course. Definitely."

He takes my reaction as hesitation for being kept in the dark. "Not big on surprises, then?"

"Surprises are fine," I say. "But the anticipation is killing me."

In more ways than one.

"Some things are worth the wait," Gabe says lightly. "The buildup is all part of the experience, isn't it? Makes for some truly mind-blowing, *deep* connection, doesn't it?"

My mouth drops open as he winks at me.

I can't help but smile at myself for walking right into that innuendo.

He clears his throat. "But we're headed to Brooklyn."

"Okay," I say.

My eyes flicker between watching his face, concentrated on the road ahead, and how beautiful the East

River and Queens look as we speed down FDR, weaving through traffic without fear of getting dents and scratches.

Without hesitation, I pull out my phone and send some pictures to Angela, who is dying to know, just as I am, what's in store for tonight.

"What's in Brooklyn?"

"You've never been to Brooklyn?" Gabe asks incredulously. "You've lived here for *how* many months now?"

I shrug. "Given the fact that I spend almost all of my free time with you, it shouldn't be that surprising. Besides, do you know how long it takes to get there on the train? Almost an hour."

"Well, it's not that much faster by car," he admits.

I sink back against the leather. "But this is infinitely less stressful than trying to get a seat or surfing the subway."

"Surfing the subway?" Gabe repeats.

"Yeah," I laugh. "I try not to touch anything for the entire ride, so I feel like I'm kind of surfing or snowboarding or doing what I can to keep my balance."

"Is that an official term?"

"I doubt I coined it, but I'm definitely using it."

"I'll have to try that next time."

"You'll need my supervision," I tell him. "There's a curve on the Q train that'll make you fall into an unsuspecting stranger if you're not careful. But I'm hoping to ride the A train all the way into Queens soon."

"Why's that?"

"Because it has the longest ride between stops near the end of the line. It's three and a half miles between the Howard Beach stop at JFK and the Broad Channel station before you hit the Rockaways." I stop and grimace. "I'm sorry. I'm probably totally boring you."

He shakes his head and squeezes my hand in reassurance. "I love a little transit trivia."

"Okay," I say, then continue regaling him with little factoids of information about transportation, some specific to New York and others I pull directly from my thesis.

He listens attentively the entire spiel and occasionally asks clarifying questions or my direct opinion on something.

I lose my train of thought as we eventually wind through a Brooklyn neighborhood, getting my first in-person glimpse at the borough.

One of the many things I love about living in New York is how quickly the scenery can change—going from my bedroom to crossing a massive bridge with skyline views, then to a busy shopping area with all different kinds of restaurants.

In Columbus, I pretty much go from downtown to the suburbs, and that's it.

Gabe expertly parks, then wraps his arm around my shoulders as he leads me down a quiet street on foot. The difference in our heights is perfect for this stance, and I love how it feels to be out somewhere with him and be touched by him.

"Almost there," he says eagerly.

The fact that he has planned something with me in mind and is legitimately happy for me to experience something makes my heart surge.

I've had boyfriends in the past, but nothing long-lasting or even remotely worth remembering when compared to

Gabe, who overshadows them so greatly, I barely remember their names at this point. I especially can't recall any notable evenings when I felt this charged just being in their presence.

Gabe stops in front of a subway entrance, smile tugging at the corner of his mouth.

I don't recognize this station, despite having spent a fair amount of time staring at the map, but it's a typical New York setup, with the dark green enclosure and stairs that lead underground.

He looks at me expectantly, waiting for me to understand the purpose of our trip here.

"You want to...surf the subway?" I ask tentatively. "Even though we drove?"

Gabe shakes his head and points to a sign ahead of us.

"Museum entrance," I whisper as the dots connect.

It's not just *any* museum—it's the one I've been absolutely dying to attend since I stumbled across its existence in grad school.

I gasp and hurry down the stairs, craning my neck to confirm my suspicion before we reach the official entrance.

"You brought me to the New York Transit Museum," I say with so much excitement that I sound more like Angela than myself right now.

Gabe grins, finally getting the reaction from me he hoped for. "It's ours for the night."

My mouth drops open. "I can't believe it."

We step up to the booth where people normally buy tickets, and a woman introduces herself as the curator of the museum.

I'm simultaneously stunned, exhilarated, and shocked

into silence by the entire experience, but I rapidly take in every single piece of information she offers up as she leads us in.

I thank Gabe at least ten times as we check out the place, and he presses a kiss on the back of my hand while we walk, keeping his attention on the curator's words.

We learn about the history of the entire transit system in New York—it has some interactive elements but mostly a lot of really cool pictures that I've never seen before—and take our time strolling along through the various exhibits and absorbing everything.

Gabe looks just as interested as I am in what the curator is saying, even though I highly doubt that's the case.

He's an actor, after all.

My favorite part of the experience is the lineup of subway cars, complete with real ads—some of which are laughably sexist—and the original, but restored, interiors. I'm amazed by the details, the different types of handrails and seats.

The curator offers to take photos of us, so we pose like we're just two normal people riding a 1910s subway to work, and we both laugh as she repeatedly presses the button on my phone, capturing my glee.

She also sheepishly asks for a picture with Gabe, explaining that her son is a big *Eggy Smith* fan, and I happily snap a few photos for her.

By the time we finish up with the rest of the tour and take a quick spin through the gift shop, where we buy a set of matching mugs, Gabe and I are both starving.

"Well, since we're in Brooklyn doing historical things,

it's only fair that we experience the best pizza New York has to offer," Gabe says as he pulls up the maps app on his phone. "That okay with you?"

"I could never say no to pizza."

Or Gabe, probably.

A few people eye him with interest when we step up to the counter.

I notice how some of them slyly take photographs, so I quickly turn my back to them in favor of gazing at all the delicious melty cheese.

"I think we should get these to go," I mumble.

He glances over his shoulder and immediately plasters a fake smile on his face, waving at a particularly giggly group of teenage girls.

"I'll sign some autographs and grab our slices if you want to avoid it and meet me in the car?" Gabe suggests, handing me the keys.

I accept his offer and slip out, watching him interact with the other customers from the tinted windows of his Lamborghini.

It's interesting to see the different age groups of people who approach him and the varying degrees of confidence with which they do it.

Unfortunately, I can't make out what exactly they're saying, but he expertly navigates the small crowd that's forming. It takes him ten minutes to make his escape, and by the time he does, two men dressed in all black and holding fancy cameras start snapping pictures.

They yell questions about me—as "Red Scarf Girl"—and he keeps his face neutral, walking quickly to the car.

I lean over and open the door for him, accepting the box of pizza on my lap so he can drive us away from this place.

"Well, that wasn't what I hoped for," he admits, checking the rearview mirror every few seconds to ensure we're not being followed.

I shake my head. "It's fine. Honestly."

Skepticism is clear in his features as he finds a place for us to pull over and dig in.

"Really," I urge. "Instead of sitting at that germ-covered table, I get to try not to get any grease on your pristine interior. I'm sure this seat is much more comfortable than the metal ones in there, anyway."

I flip open the lid, letting the scent of herbs and delicious pizza fill the car.

He relents and picks up a slice, folding it like I've seen most New Yorkers do, and takes a bite.

"I had a really good time tonight," I say after I eat almost half of a monstrous piece.

Gabe holds his hand up to his mouth. "Me too," he says.

"Thank you so much for taking me there," I say to him for probably the hundredth time. "I can't imagine it was exciting for you."

"It was pretty cool," he admits. "And now I can counter your transit facts with my own."

I laugh at that and use a napkin to clean off my fingers. "Every girl's dream. Or, at least, this girl's."

He smiles. "You ready?"

"Sure," I say evenly, not exactly sure if he intends to continue on our evening somewhere else.

"I don't want to be presumptuous or anything…" Gabe

trails off as he begins the drive back toward Manhattan. "But Zoe is at my dad's house in Connecticut tonight."

I'm about to ask what she's doing there when I pick up on what he really means. "Oh."

Gabe flutters his fingers over the steering wheel. "Is that a good 'oh' or a bad one?"

I pop a piece of cinnamon gum into my mouth. "A very, very good one," I assure him. "Great, even."

FOURTEEN

We barely make it to the bedroom.

Hell, I'm impressed that we manage to make it out of the elevator and then pause long enough for him to unlock the door.

Gabe was right earlier—the buildup to this moment has only heightened the experience of it, and as content as I am just to feel him, I need more.

And I need it now.

The doorframe of his bedroom cuts into my back as he presses himself into me and his tongue massages mine with a crushing rhythm that's simultaneously overwhelming and not enough.

This isn't just a hungry kiss—this is possession, a physical manifesto that acknowledges the feelings neither of us has dared to speak out loud. It's too early to vocalize that kind of stuff, but it feels just right to succumb to the movement between us.

"Julianna," he says huskily, then peppers kisses along my mouth and down to my neck, where he grazes the sensitive skin with his teeth.

I arch my back, pressing my body even more into his, then he abruptly pulls back, leaving me confused and breathless.

He steps fully into the room, then comes to a stop next to his massive bed.

"Care to join me?" Gabe asks.

It's a simple question, but I know there's more to it than that.

Somehow breaking this physical barrier between us signifies something deeper we're establishing here, and even if it's not too late to back out of this exact moment, I'm already *in* on Gabe King.

The rest is just inevitable.

I cross the room quickly, practically launching myself at him.

He captures my mouth again and moves my arms up, locking them around his neck so he has access to explore more of me.

His hands cup my cheeks, then my neck, and as he wanders down over my breasts, I curse myself for wearing a thick sweater.

"Need to feel more," I say, locking a leg around his waist to increase the friction.

I think I could orgasm without even taking my clothes off. But why test that theory when the alternative is within my grasp?

I claw at the buttons on his shirt, then wiggle them

open so I can feel his skin and trace the lines of his muscles.

The deep groan from the back of his throat encourages me to continue on. And so boldly—by my standards—I dip lower, tracing the line of his erection straining against his jeans.

We both shudder as I thumb the impressive number of inches, and then we're a mess of hungry kisses as we rock our bodies against each other.

The transition to being unclothed is not as seamless as it should be because we're unable to break apart long enough to remove articles of clothing.

His willpower is stronger than mine is, apparently, because once the backs of my knees hit the bedframe, he steps back.

He doesn't break eye contact as he undoes the rest of his buttons, letting his shirt flutter to the ground, or when his hands move to his belt, undoing it swiftly.

I swallow, and the sound is loud in my ears, adding to the soundtrack of my beating heart.

In a blink, Gabe is undressed save for his boxer briefs, and my mouth waters at the sight of his body that's completely bared to me.

"Julianna," he says, his voice a little gravelly. "It's your turn."

I meet his eyes, seeing the pure hunger in them, and lick my lips slowly, gathering my courage to continue. I grab the hem of my sweater with shaky hands and lift it over my head in one swoop, letting it drop onto the pile of Gabe's discarded clothes.

He inhales sharply at the sight of my exposed upper

half, then as if he can't contain himself, he runs his hands over the material of my bra.

Lace was definitely a good choice.

I undo my jeans, proudly showing off the fact that I match.

Gabe helps me step out of the rest of my clothing, a brief gentle moment between us that I like almost as much as I enjoy getting ravaged by him.

As he stands upright, he brushes his fingers over the scar on my leg, then my thighs, making me squirm, and finally, they land on the edge of my thong.

I gasp as he swipes his hand underneath the black material, letting his middle finger explore the apex of my thighs.

"You're absolutely soaked."

I can barely form a coherent thought, let alone words.

"Fuck, Julianna," he groans, gaze shooting upward.

I grab his chin, tilting his head back down so I can run my tongue over his.

We fall back on the bed, limbs twisted together.

Gabe crushes his body into mine, putting pressure in all the right places.

Although I miss his stubble, his smooth skin moving over me feels divine. I writhe against him as he sucks my nipple through the fabric, and the pressure between my legs builds.

"Gabe," I finally say, completely breathless. "Condom."

He pulls back, teetering on the edge of...something I can't quite put my finger on.

Regardless, I'm dying to see him completely fall apart, and I am absolutely done waiting.

I undo the hook of my bra under Gabe's heated gaze,

then nearly tear my thong apart as I wrench it down my legs.

"Condom," I tell him more forcefully.

He breaks out of his stupor to nod, then rifles through the pile to locate his jeans, swiping a square packet from his wallet.

I watch him slide off his boxer briefs and roll on the condom, and when he strokes his entire length, I freeze, wholly mesmerized by the movement.

Then, in a flash, he's over me.

I wrap my legs around his waist, panting at the thought of what's about to happen.

"Gabe," I urge, rolling my hips toward him.

But he's holding back, searching my face to see if there's any hesitation about this.

I sigh in frustration and move my hand down, getting a feel of him for myself, and moan as I guide his cock to my entrance.

A low growl emits from his throat, and he moves, pinning my hands up above my head as he surges into me.

I cry out in pleasure and a little bit of pain, feeling full in a way I've never experienced before—even the slightest movements threaten to completely undo me.

"Fuck," Gabe breathes.

I lock my ankles around his back, trying to hold on for the ride as he picks up the pace.

Each thrust should break me apart, but somehow, it brings us closer together, building up and up and up again.

Of course it's this good with him.

Our mouths reunite in sloppy, urgent kisses, and he

releases his grip on my hands so he can hold himself up with one while tangling the other in my hair.

I move my hips, meeting his crushing pace as best I can.

Every muscle in my body tenses as the pressure between my legs builds, and soon enough, I give in, yelling his name as my orgasm hits in a delicious explosion that I swear I feel everywhere, from the roots of my hair that Gabe tugs on all the way down to my curling toes.

He starts to slow down, breathing heavy breaths against my skin, and lavishes me with slow, delicious strokes as I come back over the edge.

"You're so damn perfect," he murmurs.

My every sense is overloaded, and I dig my fingernails into his back, trying to ground myself against him.

"Oh," he groans, slamming into me once again.

His eyes stay on mine as the line on his forehead deepens, and he bites his bottom lip as he finds his own release in just a few thrusts.

He holds himself up as his breathing returns to a normal cadence, something I have yet to figure out how to do for myself.

"That was—" Words fail me at this moment.

He smiles. "Agreed."

Gabe presses a light kiss on my lips before he pulls out and slips off the condom, tying it in a knot before throwing it away.

I reach for him, uncaring that we're a little sweaty and wound up because even though we just had sex—*really* good sex, I might add—I want more intimacy.

And when I glance at Gabe, I know I've got it.

We're facing each other, knees knocking together with

our heads resting on his fluffy white pillows, and it gives me an unobstructed view of him.

The *real* him.

It's what I've been chasing for almost as long as I've known him.

Tonight was a good reminder of how most people see him—merely a celebrity who signed up for a life of interruptions and people intruding on normal, everyday moments to ask for a photo or an autograph.

They see him as Eggy or a cologne advertisement, but even in the few months since I've started to get to know him, I can see there's so much more to him than that. I see how hard he works, how kind he is to everyone who wants his attention, and how overwhelmed he can be.

I think of all the moments he's had to spend alone, keeping his heart guarded, and I ache for him.

Tears spring to my eyes, not because I'm in pain or embarrassed or anything but because of all the emotion that is quickly building up.

In some ways, I feel like we've barely scratched the surface of our relationship, but that doesn't stop the mess of feelings from rolling in as he lazily runs his fingers through my hair.

I didn't set out to fall for him.

It just kind of happened, and there are so many consequences to consider—not just how his career requires him to be gone for months at a time, but the public scrutiny of taking our relationship to the next step.

Or if he even wants a relationship.

Once I'm certain my voice won't betray how I'm feeling,

I speak up. "Can I ask you a couple of questions?" I whisper.

"Anything," he says seriously.

I want to ask him if I'm the real deal, opening up a conversation about all those pesky feelings that need sorting through, but I chicken out.

He watches me expectantly, so I ask the first question that pops into my head.

"What is it like to be famous?"

It's one I'm sure he's been asked hundreds of times, but I don't want his prepared, surface-level answer, and he knows it.

Gabe traces my cupid's bow, giving himself time to piece together the raw truth.

I catch his thumb between my teeth and release it when he grins.

"In some ways, it's totally normal because for most of my life, random people have come up to me in the streets, proposing to me or asking me inappropriate questions, so I've gotten used to it," he admits. "It's nothing out of the ordinary."

"Just because it's not out of the ordinary doesn't mean that it's something you want to be your version of normal," I hypothesize.

He nods. "When I was in my early twenties, I loved it. Jumping the line to get into clubs and bars, scoring invites to exclusive parties, and going on free press trips all in exchange for letting myself be photographed."

"That doesn't seem like the Gabe I know."

"It got old eventually, and I'm actually pretty ashamed of my behavior back then." He takes a deep breath. "And unfortunately for me, it's all well-documented in headlines and photos that are now forever preserved online for anyone to see. My fans—god, that sounds so pretentious to say—but my fans are amazing for the most part."

"'For the most part' isn't exactly comforting."

"I've learned to love them in my own way, I guess. If you look at my tagged photos on any platform, it's a little...overwhelming. And slightly terrifying. I've been manipulated into so many different pictures and videos, and there have been thousands of stories written about Melanie and me that I'm a little desensitized to it at this point."

"I know you told me that the two of you have only been friends, but...there's really no story with you and Melanie? Everyone just goes off what was in the movies?"

That makes him chuckle.

I quirk an eyebrow and wait for him to continue.

"It's almost embarrassing to talk about this while naked. She's like my second sister, honestly. This huge fandom was built on us being a couple in *Eggy*, and it never really died down. Plus, every single answer we gave in an interview is somewhere online, meaning that when she hinted about having a crush on me when we were thirteen, people use that to create some sort of long, unrequited love story between the two of us. Her fiancée and I laugh about it endlessly, much to Melanie's annoyance."

"She's getting married?"

"They keep putting off the actual wedding because of their schedules, but it'll happen eventually," he says. "Ruby is the best. She's hilarious, and I know you two will hit it off next time they're in town."

I don't get the feeling that Melanie will want to let me "in" enough to meet her fiancée, but I keep that thought to myself.

"For now, they're trying to figure out if they should have a big 'coming out,' or just drop the news casually after they get married, or wait to see if pictures get leaked from their honeymoon in Prague."

"Prague?" I ask. "I thought most people went somewhere luxurious and beachy for a honeymoon?"

"I wouldn't know," he says, pressing a quick kiss on my lips. "But when I get married and go on my honeymoon, I'll let you know how it turns out."

I laugh, forcing myself not to get carried away with that by pivoting to another question. "If you could do anything in the world or go anywhere you want, what would you pick?"

He moves closer, almost so our noses touch, and runs his hand down my spine. "I would be right here, with you."

Damn.

He's good.

A warm feeling encircles my entire body at his words.

"But I've been fooled before, Julianna," he says. "Approached and manipulated so many times that for a while, it made me cynical."

His words don't surprise me, given his reaction when we first met.

And it's absolutely wild to me to consider that we went from being total strangers, stumbling into each other by chance, to two people who are baring themselves and their souls to each other.

"I just need to know," Gabe continues, eyes intense. "Are you the real deal?"

I drag my fingertips up along his arm, trying to memorize every groove and line of muscle. "I'd like to be," I admit to him.

I watch the smile tug at the corner of his mouth until he gives into it completely, then he pulls me on top of him and we get lost—and found—in each other once again.

FIFTEEN

We spend the next hour talking and lazily kissing until we both start to nod off.

"I should probably head downstairs," I say reluctantly because I never want to leave this bed.

He frowns. "Okay. I'll walk you."

I dress gingerly, already knowing I'm going to be sore from head to toe tomorrow from the different positions we tried out during our second round. But for some reason, I'm thrilled to have a physical reminder of our time together, like each step forward releases a dose of Gabe serotonin in my mind.

I'm content to live in bliss now, but as we continue on in our relationship, eventually we're going to have to face whatever backlash comes along with it. I just hope at that point I'll have a hold on my life, and we'll have a stronger place in each other's.

But deep in the back of my mind, I'm aware that this stage of our relationship is a ticking clock—not just because it's new and exciting, like most are in this phase, but because in January, Gabe's off to Australia for his next movie.

I can't even remember where he goes after that, but I don't know if four months of a relationship will be enough to hold up to something long-distance, or if we'll even want that.

We need time to get situated, to explore this thing between us before we let the rest of the world in. Also, it's too early to discuss things like that, so I just have to hope nothing comes out before we are ready to handle it together—along with his PR person.

For the time being, I'm more than content to keep Gabe King all to myself.

"Are you sure you don't want to stay over?" he asks me once we've reached the Finch family's front door.

"I definitely *do,*" I retort, wrapping my arms around his neck. "But it's probably better if I make an appearance here tonight."

Gabe knows that I absolutely do not love my job, but I haven't exactly shared the details of how overbearing Amanda can be...or how possessive Peter gets. I'm hoping to handle it on my own until it's no longer an issue or I've found employment elsewhere.

But of course, it's Peter who opens the door after Gabe has captured my lips and pulled me into him, his final attempt to coerce me into heading back.

He clears his throat impatiently, and I reluctantly break away from Gabe.

I try to smooth my appearance, like his interrupting

isn't jarring, but my hair is in a tremendous rat's nest from our earlier activities and my shirt is a wrinkled disaster.

"Hi, Peter," Gabe says immediately, extending a hand to shake. "I'm Gabe."

Peter looks him up and down, sensing familiarity but unable to place it.

"He's our neighbor," I explain.

"And Julianna's boyfriend," Gabe adds, making us both break out into smiles.

Peter reluctantly shakes his hand. "It's a little late, isn't it? For hallway activities?"

It's nearly midnight, but it's not like I have a curfew or anything—after all, I'm not a child, and he is certainly not my father or guardian.

I think those same thoughts flash in Gabe's mind, too, but he keeps up his friendly mask.

I guess it's a gift that he's so well practiced in keeping his distance from people and not letting their comments get to him, but it's not a trait I share.

Plus, the crash from complete bliss to full-fledged irritation is not one I wanted to experience, heightening my frustration at the situation and with Peter.

"I'll see you later, Julianna." Gabe drops a kiss on my cheek before he heads back toward the stairs. "Nice to meet you, Peter."

I watch him walk away and seriously consider following him, especially when Peter scoffs at his politeness.

All I want to do right now is shower and fall right into a deep sleep, catching as many hours as I can before Will or Angela decides to wake me up early, asking for breakfast or demanding details about my date, but Peter waves me into the apartment and toward the couch.

I oblige him, even though I really don't want to.

"This is unacceptable behavior," he snaps before I even get settled. "Staying out all hours of the night, not to mention how inappropriate it is for you to be doing *that* in our hallway. What if our neighbors saw? What if my *son* saw?"

I don't say what I really think, which is that it probably would be weird for Will to see adults expressing affection instead of treating each other like business associates, and that given that Will plays video games with Gabe at least twice a week, I think he'd be fine with it.

But I know voicing either of those things will get me in trouble, so I don't say anything.

"If you keep this up, we'll have no choice but to fire you," Peter threatens.

I should defend myself—not only is he wrong but this entire conversation is incredibly inappropriate.

Peter has made me feel uncomfortable nearly every moment I've been in his presence since I accepted this job. As much as I cling to my nannying gig for the safety, security, money, and housing it provides, it's not worth compromising my sanity to please the whims of an unhappily married couple.

In lieu of opening my mouth and getting myself fired on the spot, I imagine I'm Gabe or Melanie, getting pestered by someone who isn't really worth my time, and I pull up my mental shields to keep myself under control.

"Okay, Peter," I say coolly.

He balks at my easy acceptance, clearly expecting me to fight back.

I think that's what he wants...an argument or some sort of passion directed toward him, but I can't find it in me to care.

"Is that all?" I ask him.

He stands up, acting like it's his idea to end our conversation. "I will see you bright and early in the morning."

"Sure," I say, then head off to my room.

I hate to wash off Gabe's scent, but Peter ruined the magic of the evening so thoroughly that I end up spending extra time scrubbing at my skin in addition to how long it takes me to get the knots out of my hair.

When I finally crawl into bed, I'm elated to see a text from Gabe.

I can't stop thinking about you.

A massive, embarrassing smile overtakes my face. *Right back at you, Mr. King.*

You okay?

More than okay, I promise him.

Me too.

But maybe we should save the kissing for your doorway...and bedroom...and kitchen...and shower, I suggest.

Shower sex?

I grin again. *Yes.*

Is it too soon for you to come back up?

I take a selfie of me in bed, curled up in an oversized sweatshirt and cocooned beneath every cover available to me. *Text you tomorrow?*

Gabe replies with a photo of himself tangled up in the sheets that I'm now very familiar with, and I'm still trying to decipher if he's shirtless or completely naked when another text from him comes through.

Sweet dreams.

I yawn as I hold my phone to my chest, hoping that I'll dream of him.

While sleep eventually does come, I'm restless, and even in my dreams, I'm fixated on Peter's absurdity instead of Gabe's deliciousness.

I take it as a bad sign when I wake up the next morning groggy and dehydrated.

And I find that instinct is correct when over the next two weeks, I barely see Gabe.

We're like passing ships, only communicating through scattered text messages because he's on night shoots while the Finches suddenly seem to need every single second of my time and attention.

In the past, I've just gone along with the whims of Amanda and Peter, having no other option, but now, because of Gabe, or the contract work I did, or my own renewed sense of self, I've reached my limit.

I can't stay here, following around a thirteen-year-old—as sweet as he is—and being treated like garbage by Amanda and Peter.

It's time to look for another job.

I should have started this process months ago, and I'm ashamed at myself for letting it go on this long.

In the brief periods I do have time to myself, usually before going to bed and texting Gabe as he gets his hair done on set, I send out applications. I get immediately rejected by most but have a few still outstanding that I haven't heard back from.

I like to imagine that my resume is being argued over by executives somewhere, but in reality, it's probably sitting in a pile with fifty others.

I'm trying not to lose hope, but it's getting more difficult each day, and I hit my lowest point on a Saturday morning at the dining table.

Will is telling me about some sort of new add-on for his game, and instead of the scent of coffee or breakfast food, my nostrils fill with a scent that I recognize but can't place.

"Does it smell like..." I pause as a shiver of disgust rolls down my spine. "Spearmint?"

"It does," Peter says proudly, sitting down beside his son and ruffling his hair.

I can tell Will absolutely hates it when he does that, but he doesn't say anything.

"Do you like it?" Peter asks, putting on false bravado.

"It's fine," I tell him evenly.

But it's not.

It's too potent and stifling, and unlike the scent of spearmint that used to follow Gabe around, this one makes me nauseous—I can't tell if it's because of all the chemicals that accompany it or because of the strange game Peter has decided to play.

I grind my teeth and grip my spoon, needing to let the anger out in some small way.

"What brand did you say this was, Amanda?" he asks his wife while eyeing me.

"It's that new Gabe King cologne," she says, sitting down with a cup of coffee in her hands. "I think it smells as delicious as he probably does."

I grind my teeth at those words.

Peter gives me a challenging look, like he's daring me to come clean about my relationship with Gabe, knowing that Amanda will have some absurd reaction to the news.

I don't give him the satisfaction that he seems desperate for in favor of politely excusing myself, dropping my dishes in the dishwasher, and hiding in my room until it's time to take Will to his piano lesson.

SIXTEEN

"So, I was thinking about Christmas this year," Angela tells me over the phone.

It's the Friday after Thanksgiving, and for once, I'm enjoying the quiet.

In the past, Angela and I spent this time together, gorging on leftovers while she read a magazine or watched something on her laptop and I studied or did some sort of activity relating to academia.

But this year, of course, I'm holed up in my bedroom, alone.

"Does Mom already have the tree up?" I ask my sister, who has been talking to me with her mouth full of turkey sandwich for the last ten minutes.

"Of course she does," Angela says after a swallow that's big enough I hear it through the phone. "I barely made it through my second slice of pumpkin pie yesterday before she started ordering Dad and me around, making us pull boxes from the attic and getting teary over the fact that you weren't there to help."

I sigh, wishing I could have been there, too.

The Finches had their Thanksgiving over lunch yesterday, and I wasn't explicitly invited or uninvited, so I just kind of awkwardly hovered in my room until Gabe and Zoe returned from dinner in Connecticut with an overwhelming amount of leftovers that I happily took off their hands.

I've always loved the holiday season, and I especially can't wait to see all the decorations around the city. Some restaurants and buildings already have lights strung up around the windows or in the landscaping—but unfortunately, Peter and Amanda aren't big into decorating.

"What would you think about me coming to see you for Christmas this year?" Angela asks.

"I think that would be amazing!" I can't hide my enthusiasm.

I wanted her to come visit in the summer, but with being so new to my job and the city, we decided it was best to push it out.

Now that I'm urgently trying to get a new job and figure my life out, I feel more bold and less invested in being the perfect, silent nanny. I do know that I'll need to clear it with them for her to stay in my room with me...or sneak her in somehow, because there's no way either of us can afford a hotel.

"Well, I'm booking a super last-minute, cheap deal for next weekend," she says casually.

"Next weekend?" I sputter to the sound of her computer mouse clicking.

"Yep, and I am...just about...done! No turning back now."

I laugh. "I can't believe you just did that."

"Well, I figured you would tell me not to book it if I put it off," Angela explains. "And this alert popped up, so I had to go for it."

"No turning back now," I say, biting back a grin.

We both chatter excitedly for a few more minutes about what we can do around the city and what she plans on wearing to "take over New York City" until I have to get ready for the day.

Peter and Amanda spend the bulk of the afternoon at a wine tasting out on Long Island with a group of friends while Will tries to teach me how to last more than two minutes in *Call of Duty*.

He's not successful in that endeavor, but we have fun.

When they return hours later, they both seem to be in a good enough mood for me to ask about my sister, and I'm surprised that they agree, then they kind of brush past the topic as if it's not a big deal.

I suppose having a blood relation in my bedroom is a little different than making out with someone against their front door.

Finally, after dinner, I'm free of the Finches for another night, so I walk up the stairs toward Gabe's place.

Zoe roped him into throwing another party—very small this time, she promised, with close friends only. Gabe reluctantly agreed to it after she threatened to collect all sorts of embarrassing pictures from their family home and show them to me and his social media followers.

After I knock, Gabe opens the door and immediately pulls me into his arms.

I'm knocked off balance, so I happily relax into him, inhaling the scent of cinnamon.

"Why does it feel like it's been forever since I've seen you?" he murmurs into my hair.

Surprisingly, it feels that way to me, too, even though it has been less than a day since I've stood in this very same spot.

That realization scares me as much as it exhilarates me that he has the same thought.

I don't get to dwell on it, though.

"God, Gabriel, at least let her inside before you maul her," Zoe says, pulling me by the arm out of our embrace.

Gabe rolls his eyes at her as she leads me toward the kitchen and does a pretty adequate job of convincing me that her Franzia cocktail isn't going to give me a headache.

When we join the group in the main room, I'm relieved that it is a much smaller group than last time.

I actually recognize most of the people here, and those I don't, Gabe quickly introduces me to, including Ruby and some of his castmates.

I settle in beside him on the couch, with his arm slung around the back of it, while Zoe perches on the arm, practically sitting in my lap, and Pancake curls up on my feet.

It makes me feel enveloped by the Kings, and I don't hate it.

"So, you're the reason behind Gabe's new gum flavor?" Ruby asks me. "The Commoners are going wild over it."

"All hail the King," Zoe says, clinking the edge of her glass with mine.

"Are they?" I ask.

Ruby nods. "Totally losing their shit. More so than when Melanie and Gabe were photographed in Hawaii a few years ago. Everyone thought he was going to propose, but...it was actually my twenty-fifth birthday trip."

I snort, then finally take a sip of the drink Zoe made. "This actually isn't that bad," I say, looking at her with a lifted brow.

Zoe rolls her eyes. "Told you so."

"So, Julianna, Gabe tells me that you're kind of a history nerd," Ruby says, trying once again to keep up the conversation.

I like that she's making an effort to get to know me.

She has these wide, approachable eyes that make me immediately want to trust her—unlike Melanie, who only regards me with trepidation, if at all.

"Well, if my student loans are any measure, then I think I deserve a gold medal in the nerd Olympics," I joke.

"Oh, god, I know," Ruby agrees, which surprises me.

"What did you study?" I ask her.

"Psychology," she laughs. "Which is obviously the most useless degree unless you go all the way, which is exactly what I did. I got my doctorate in clinical psychology last year, and I'll be paying it off until I'm sixty, I swear."

I consider what Gabe said about me being down-to-earth, coupled with the fact that he said I would like Ruby. Part of me wonders if he thinks we can relate because we're, well...poor.

It could be because we both had the gumption to follow our passion, despite the financial burden, and we both spend lots of time in New York City—and, on top of all that, we both date someone who requires great compromise.

Regardless, he's right, and I'm well on my way to enjoying her company.

"Plus, I went to only private colleges," Ruby groans.

"Oh no," I sympathize. "I had my heart set on Ohio University for a long time, but I ended up going to OSU because it was so much more affordable. Plus, my dad loves the football team there, so I was able to use my student discount to buy his Christmas gifts every year."

"Well, I think you're both great and smart, even if you have negative net worths," Zoe teases us.

Ruby laughs. "Said like a true influencer with a trust fund from her famous brother."

Zoe glares at her with mock indignation. "Well, I guess I won't be getting any free therapy sessions from you."

They continue back and forth, their banter clearly built on years of inside jokes and teasing, so I lean into Gabe slightly, calling his attention back to me.

He wraps his arm around my shoulders tighter to pull me in and kiss my temple. "You having fun?"

I nod. "Yeah, Ruby's great."

It's kind of weird to be at a party again, surrounded by potential friends. It hasn't happened much since my undergraduate days, and even then, it wasn't really my normal scene.

"Are you coming, Julianna?" Josh asks.

"To what?"

"The premiere of *The Frozen Ignition.*"

"It's what we were all just talking about," Gabe explains. "Josh did the set design for this movie, and he's begging us all to clear our schedules next weekend to make an appearance."

I'm flattered that he's asked me to join, but given everything Gabe and I discussed recently about our relationship, I don't think it's appropriate.

"My sister is coming up next weekend," I say, thankful to have an excuse to bow out.

"That's great," Gabe says. "I can't wait to meet her."

"Then you can *both* come to my premiere," Josh pushes.

"I don't think that's the best idea," I tell him, shifting uncomfortably.

He balks. "Why not?"

I look to Gabe, who gives me a nod, signaling that these people can be trusted.

"Well, Gabe and I aren't ready to announce our relationship to the world yet—"

"What?" Melanie gasps, then catches herself, resuming the cold, stoic state that I'm getting more familiar with.

Her tight smile doesn't reveal if she's surprised or outraged by this news, but Gabe doesn't seem fazed by her reaction.

"We're going to hold on to our little bubble for as long as we can," Gabe tells them.

"And what does this have to do with my premiere?" Josh cuts in. "It's not like you two have to makeout on the red carpet."

We all laugh at that, except Zoe, who wrinkles her nose in disgust.

"Yes, because no one on the internet will make the connection that one of the two random girls showing up with us to an event could possibly be the Red Scarf Girl," Zoe snaps at him.

Josh considers her words. "Well, how about *you guys* all walk the carpet and sit with me, and Julianna and her sister…" He looks to me.

"Angela," I prompt.

"Julianna and Angela can attend and sit nearby, and then we can all go to the afterparty together."

Gabe looks at me and shrugs, signaling that it's my choice.

I smile. "Angela's going to die when I tell her."

"Is that a yes?" Josh says excitedly.

"Sure," I say, but he's already firing off emails to people, arranging for tickets and seating and whatnot.

Pancake sits up and rests her snout on my knees so I can scratch behind her ears, somehow sensing that I need to be grounded into reality.

I'm more than content to sit back and watch the conversation happen around me, but I'm actually not silent for too long because someone has a question for me or pulls me into a conversation or in some way requires my attention.

I feel comfortable with this group, and I'm happy to see that Gabe does, too. It's his small circle of trustworthy friends that he doesn't have to put up a front for. They all tease one another and reminisce, filling me in on details of stories I don't understand; although, I laugh right along with them.

After my second glass of Zoe's punch, I excuse myself to go to the bathroom.

I'm feeling just a little bit tipsy, so as I wash my hands, I resolve to cut myself off and take a swish of mouthwash, knowing it will ruin the taste enough for me to not be tempted.

I don't care what Zoe promises. A third glass of sugary wine is not a good idea. I head to the kitchen to grab myself a glass of water.

"Oh," I say, jumping back before I run smack into Melanie. "Sorry."

Her arms are folded on her chest like she's purposely being closed off and intimidating, but I see through it.

I am, however, curious as to why she's deliberately cornering me in the hallway.

"Are you okay?" I ask her.

She lets out a big, long dramatic sigh. "Look, I know I haven't been...the warmest to you, and I am sorry if I made you feel uncomfortable."

I don't prompt her next set of words or try and help her train of thought along—whatever words are buried inside her right now need to come out by her own doing, regardless of how painful they will be for me to hear.

"I've just seen Gabe get hurt over the years. Like, really hurt, and not just by girlfriends but by even friends or colleagues, and I'm just a little slow to open up to new people."

I nod in understanding.

If I were in her expensive shoes, I'd be skeptical, too.

There are millions of girls vying for Gabe's attention, and she's not sure what makes me different—or at least, I hope even though she didn't when we first met that she does now.

"Maybe that makes me come off as a bitch, but more

often than not, my protective instincts are usually valid. It's just, now that I understand you're not going away, I feel obligated to warn you."

"Warn me?" I say. "About what?"

She offers me a look of pity. "Whether giving up your entire life is worth spending it with him."

I step back, needing just a small reprieve from her scrutiny.

"Gabe is the best, frankly, and I'm sure what you two have is very special. But you're going to need to take a hard look at your life and decide if the public scrutiny, the fan mobs, the weeks or months away from each other—"

She stops suddenly, like she's pulling inspiration from an open wound.

And that's when it hits me.

It's not necessarily me she has an issue with, but she seems to be projecting all of her inner struggles and conflicts in her relationship with Ruby on me.

Her concerns are valid, but she doesn't know me enough to understand that I've already done the mental modeling of this situation and imagined my life without him.

"He's worth it," I say confidently.

Melanie's eyes flash in surprise at my tone.

"When you...love someone," I start, stumbling slightly over that four-letter word. "It's my personal belief that you'll do anything for them. In this case, I think any backlash about celebrating a relationship is par for the course, but it's not worth giving up everything for it. It's tougher than *normal* circumstances, sure, but doesn't that make it all worth it? That there's something so special happening that it's worth fighting for?"

She chews on her bottom lip, contemplating my words.

"And I'm sure that Ruby feels the same way," I add quietly.

Melanie tightens her arms across her body, not because she's angry but because she feels like she's holding her defenses together.

If I knew her better, I'd probably offer words of comfort or maybe even pull her into a hug, but I just stand silently, waiting for her to process, until Gabe approaches.

"Everything okay in here?" Gabe asks, warily eyeing the two of us.

Melanie takes a deep breath, then she offers us a genuine smile.

"Fine," Melanie says, voice a little higher than I've heard it. "Everything's going to be just fine."

I nod, then slip my hand into his, hoping that will actually be true.

SEVENTEEN

"You are living a dream life," my sister says to me as we walk around Washington Square Park. "I mean, look at this place."

She gestures to the marble arch, framed by trees hung with leaves in all their late fall glory, then to the groups of people enjoying what is usually a fountain in the summer but currently serves as a seating area for buskers, families, and tourists.

It's one of the places I stumbled upon in the city during one of my Bagel Friday walks on Mary's recommendation. Although it's less crowded and bustling now than it was in the summer months, I understand the appeal.

There's something magical about stumbling across places that serve as an intersection of art, nature, and culture.

"I do love it here," I tell her. "But it's not like I spend my days wandering around shopping and sitting in parks."

Which is exactly what we have been doing all morning.

"Oh, I'm very familiar," Angela reminds me. "It has been nice to see your pictures have more people in them recently, though. You have *friends* now. And a *celebrity boyfriend*."

"Do I?" I tease. "Red Scarf Girl could be anyone, really."

She tightens her reclaimed scarf around her neck and smirks. "I cannot wait to meet Gabe tonight."

If I had my preference, we would have a quiet night in, or maybe go out to dinner just the three of us, but when I told Angela about the premiere, she nearly lost her mind with excitement and insisted that we find trendy new outfits in the city before the event.

"We'd better catch the train back uptown if we want to get ready in time," I say after I check the time on my phone.

"You sure you don't want to tell me more facts about the history of the arch or the very specific type of marble that was used to build it? Oh, what about how it was originally constructed—"

"Maybe I should leave you here to fend for yourself instead," I huff.

She rolls her eyes at my annoyance, then we set off in the direction of the subway entrance, weighed down with our new dresses—scored at a little boutique having a closing sale—and new pair of shoes for her.

"So, when are you planning to tell Mom and Dad about Gabe?" Angela asks once we're through the turnstiles.

I want to tell her about the history of how the subway stations changed over the years—which I got a firsthand look at in the trip to the Transit Museum—but I settle for actually answering her question.

“I haven’t figured out how to do it yet,” I admit.

“Well, you better do it soon because they’re going to want to see pictures and, more than that, the truth about what you’re up to.”

I sigh. “Are you sure you don’t want to tell them for me?”

“Absolutely not,” she says immediately. “It’s going to be weird enough for them that you’re dating someone seriously, not to mention that...it’s him.”

“I know—”

“No,” Angela cuts me off. “It’s *him*.”

I catch a glimpse of Gabe’s cologne ad tacked up on the tile wall and sigh. At least no one has defaced it yet.

She cackles. “You had sex with a man whose face is plastered all around Manhattan!”

“Keep it down, Ang,” I scold, even though no one is paying any attention to us.

One perk of living in such a busy, crowded city is that no one really cares who you are because they’re trying to get wherever they’re going and are wrapped up in their own set of problems.

I know that’s why Gabe likes it here so much—most of the time he can live with some sense of anonymity.

But he still, occasionally, gets mobbed by fans outside press events, which is yet another reason I’m dreading tonight.

In theory, it will be fun to get more of a glimpse into his world and all the glamour, but most of all, I just want to see how he is in it. I like spending time with Gabe, and part of that is seeing how he reacts to certain situations and handles himself.

Angela and I always got ready for high school dances together, and this seems like a more adult version of it.

She spent most of the morning drilling me with questions I'm unable to answer, demanding to know who will be at the premiere and what the afterparty will be like, even though she'll have a blast no matter what we do.

My sister is the type of person who could have fun in the middle of a field with no one to talk to.

I envy her optimism and excitement for all facets of life; sometimes, I wish I shared that trait.

She's more like my dad, the happy-go-lucky guy who gambles and has a repertoire of inappropriate jokes to share at a moment's notice, while my mom and I are more of an introverted, planner type.

That's not to say my sister doesn't have it together, though, because she already has a job lined up with a marketing agency in Columbus where she interned last summer.

I'm ridiculously proud of her, even though I'm secretly hoping that she'll eventually want to move up to New York.

When we finally get back to the apartment, Peter, Amanda, and Will are nowhere to be found.

They were nice enough to Angela when she arrived last night, and I was grateful for that. Still, I'd rather not tiptoe around the apartment and argue with Angela in whispers over my hair and makeup.

We take turns showering and blow-drying our hair. Then Angela cranks up music to set the mood, and we spend the next two hours getting ready, laughing and joking as we fight over the bathroom mirror.

She's been dying to try out magnetic false eyelashes,

which kind of terrify me, so I'm full of admiration when she successfully gets them on.

A few days ago, Zoe sent me some pictures of her past premiere looks. Even though Angela and I won't be photographed or paid any attention, we wanted to feel fancy and fit in with the rest of the group as best we can after the movie.

I think we've pulled it off.

Angela looks stunning in a vintage, beaded, cream-colored dress, paired with sky-high heels that make me nervous just watching her walk in, while I wear a silky black dress that she pressured me into buying with some of the money from the project with Josh.

I can't wait to see Gabe all dressed up again. Frankly, it's a real shame he doesn't permanently walk around in 1920s attire.

When I get the notification that the car Gabe arranged for Angela and me has arrived, we give each other a once-over before we head downstairs, then we crawl through traffic all the way to Lincoln Center.

On a regular day, this area is busy, but currently, with the coordination of cars and the number of people milling around, it's total *madness*.

We barely force our way through the crowd to get to the little tented off will-call area to get our tickets.

"This is insane," Angela says.

I don't disagree with her, but her tone implies that she finds it cool or impressive, whereas I just want to get the hell away from it as fast as I can. I don't think her gaze has stopped moving since we got out of the car.

I grab her by the wrist and lead her toward the

entrance, and once inside, we gratefully accept glasses of champagne from a server who is carrying them on a damn silver platter.

We pause for a beat and sip from our glasses, giving my ears some time to recover from all the screaming outside while Angela's busy taking in the scene.

Eventually, we wander around the room a little bit, then make our way over to the floor-to-ceiling windows to check out the chaos below.

From our vantage point, we can see the red carpet from start to finish, lined with photographers and taped-off interview areas. Over the years, Angela has forced me to watch a few of these events on television, usually leading up to some big award show.

"So, this is what it looks like from the other side," I say, watching a few people laugh and pose.

It looks really awkward to me, but they have mastered the art of dealing with flashing photography and casual-yet-forced stances.

Angela hums appreciatively as she takes a sip. "Could be you down there someday, you know."

I frown at that thought.

"Don't tell me you haven't thought about it," Angela scoffs.

"I have," I admit. "But just thinking about all that attention makes me want to pass out."

"Why? You're the most beautiful woman here."

I smile at her compliment, trying to mask my inner turmoil.

Last weekend, when Melanie approached me in the hallway, I stood my ground with her, making it clear that I cared enough about Gabe to deal with the fallout, but in the days that followed, her concerns festered in my mind.

And now, I'm ready to let it all spill out, getting confirmation that I'm making the right decision from the person who knows me better than anyone.

"It's just...I don't know. You've seen how ruthlessly the press treat Gabe and Melanie, and that's all speculation. What would happen if we suddenly went public? Imagine all the scrutiny and rumors."

"So don't look at it," Angela suggests dismissively.

"But it's there."

"Who cares?"

I glare at her. "You're being pretty nonchalant about this."

"And you're being stupid."

"Good argument, Ang," I snap at her.

"I'm just saying who *cares* who is judging you for how you live your life? Isn't being with him worth having a few pictures taken or dealing with strangers saying dumb stuff that you don't even have to experience if you don't *want* to?"

My sister has never been the most eloquent, but I know she's right and that she just wants the best for me.

That reminder makes me focus on the scene below with a new perspective.

Could I imagine myself trailing alongside Gabe and laughing with Zoe while he's pulled into interviews? Would a picture of us circulating online be the worst thing to happen? Would speculation about our relationship and opening ourselves up to public scrutiny be as bad as I'm imagining?

I don't have time to answer my own questions because the crowd noise below picks up exponentially, and Angela squeals beside me.

"There he is," she says, pointing him out as if I can't see him with my own eyes.

Gabe steps up to the carpet with Zoe on his arm.

Rina trails closely behind, making sure they're posing correctly, and coordinates their stops along the carpet with various people in all black and wearing headsets.

Angela and I sip our drinks as we watch the pair's progress, posing together then separately before they're both pulled into different interviews.

They're all smiles, and I know they're turning up the charm and gushing about the film and Josh, even though they haven't seen it yet.

"Come on, let's take a selfie together," Angela says, grabbing my phone and holding it up to capture us with Gabe in the background.

After another glass of champagne and more photos and people-watching, we find our seats.

All the stars and everyone involved with the film's production slowly fill up the first floor, while Angela and I sit on the balcony in the front row, which seems to be reserved for fans and the press.

Angela points out various celebrities who are coming in to take their seats.

It's a little bit like we're watching animals at a zoo, and it makes me feel strange, but everyone else around us is gawking, too, so at the very least, I can take comfort in that.

My phone vibrates in my palm, and I smile when I see Gabe's name pop up.

Did you two get in okay?

"Ooh, is that Loverboy?" Angela asks, leaning over to read his message. "Send him the picture we took."

I oblige and wait for his response.

"There he is."

Gabe walks in with a group, using the other people to shield him from getting trapped in conversations. Before he takes his seat beside Zoe, he glances up at me and smiles, which I return easily.

The group of girls behind Angela and me squeal with delight, thinking he's acknowledging their presence, and then I'm stuck listening to them run through the latest gossip about him and gush over his performance in his most recent movie until the current one begins.

EIGHTEEN

"You look gorgeous," Gabe says as he slides a hand around my waist.

Finally, after the torture of watching him from afar this evening, I get to enjoy the feeling of him holding me close.

I sigh in relief, relaxing my back against his chest.

"I could barely concentrate on the movie," he whispers after pressing a kiss to my temple. "Don't tell Josh that, though."

"Your secret is safe with me," I tell him, chuckling slightly.

"Hello," Angela calls, stepping closer to us with three topped-off champagne flutes. "I come bearing gifts."

I've lost track of how many glasses I've drank, mostly just to have something to keep my hands occupied with at this afterparty, but I'm feeling pretty good.

Gabe offers her one of his signature smiles. "You must be Angela."

She's momentarily blinded by how alluring he is in

person, but she composes herself. "You look familiar," she teases. "Have we met before?"

He laughs, and they hug in greeting.

"I thought you would smell like spearmint gum," Angela says after stepping back.

I groan. "Not you, too. Unlike me, my sister had a pretty big thing for Eggy back in the day," I explain to Gabe.

Her eyes go wide. "Jules, you can't just tell him that."

"Why not?" I balk, then take a sip of champagne.

She aggressively blinks at me like I'm an idiot for not understanding. "I'm trying to make a good first impression here."

Gabe laughs. "I think I'm the one who needs to make a good first impression. First meeting of the girlfriend's family. Actually, I should introduce you to..."

While he turns and waves Zoe over, Angela mouths *girlfriend* to me with exaggerated excitement.

"Angela!" Zoe calls, pulling her into an easy embrace.

"Oh my gosh, Zoe," Angela practically squeals. "It's so great to meet you. Finally!"

The two of them start chatting like old friends—something that confuses Gabe and me—leaving us to step back and watch as they gush over each other's outfits and talk excitedly about the movie and the event.

I've long thought that Zoe reminded me of Angela, but seeing them interact is kind of odd.

They're total opposites in appearance but nearly identical in mannerism, which is confirmed when they start taking pictures in matching poses without planning it.

"Well, this is mildly terrifying," I admit. "Angela is enough to handle on her own."

"So is my sister," Gabe says, then scans the room around us. "Do you want to walk around? Hide somewhere? Dance? Meet some people?"

"I should stay away from Josh," I tell him.

Gabe smirks. "Why? What'd you see in the film that's going to ruin his night?"

"Flaws in some of the dialogue," I say with a frown. "I get that it's supposed to be a fun movie, but you can't build a space world with its own races and languages, then use modern jokes. Like in the scene where Captain Tor is acting like he dialed the wrong number just to mess with General Bloot. They're on spaceships, not using a rotary phone. I know it's not directly tied to his work, but...I don't know. It irked me."

Gabe laughs. "I'm suddenly grateful that you haven't seen any of my movies."

"I doubt I'd be able to focus on stuff like that if you were on the screen," I say slyly.

He runs his hands along my sides, gripping the fabric of my dress. "I know the feeling."

I slide my hands up his chest, fingers gliding along the smooth lapels of his suit jacket.

"I've missed you," Gabe says, tilting his head down.

"None of that," Zoe snaps. "Well, here at least. Come on."

She tugs me along while holding her vape pen between her teeth.

"Have you ever wished you were an only child?" I ask Gabe as I'm pulled in her wake.

He sighs as he follows. "Never more than at this moment."

The next hour passes with Zoe saving Gabe and me from ourselves.

Although this is a private event and there are no official photographers, I see enough people taking pictures and videos on their cellphones to make me a little nervous.

But my sister thrives in this setting. Angela isn't a hit with just Zoe—she talks to Gabe, Josh, and other party-goers with an ease I wish I possessed.

She somehow has a relatable story for every single topic, even keeping up with Gabe and the director of the film for a ten-minute conversation about the Yankees. I don't think my sister has ever watched a baseball game in her life.

Still, I enjoy myself in my own way.

As much as I prefer to stay in, I'm relishing how nice it is to be dressed up and socializing...but that might only be because Gabe keeps sending fiery gazes my way, then brushing up against me while we're in conversations with people.

We eventually make our way to the dancefloor for a few songs, and thankfully, it's not like the club dancing I experienced in college—it's almost like a group dance, where we all jump around and belt out the lyrics but end up laughing more than anything.

I'm also delighted that Gabe is an absolutely terrible singer.

It's not that I take joy in him not having a talent but because it's another detail I've discovered about him, a little flaw that I'm keeping to myself.

When Angela and Zoe declare that they want to jet off to another club to meet guys and *actually* dance, Gabe and I take our cue to leave.

"Are you sure you want to go out?" I ask Angela. "We have such a short time together, and I want to see you as much as I can—"

"You following me around is going to be more annoying than anything else," she says. "Zoe and I will be fine on our own. I'll see you later if you're still up."

I hesitate slightly.

"Go home with your man," Angela demands.

And so I do.

The ride to his apartment is fast, but when we get in, our movements are slow.

We take our time, lavishing each other with the affection and attention we've sorely missed these past few weeks.

"I wish we could do this every single day," Gabe says before he kisses me softly.

His words, said so nonchalantly, change everything.

Rather, they set off a series of thoughts in my mind I hadn't allowed myself to grow attached to until he vocalized them, and it's at this moment I know that's what I, too, wish for when we're apart.

Enveloped in the scent of cinnamon, I find complete contentment in just kissing him on the couch, like we're two teenagers exploring and clinging to each other while ignoring the rest of the world around us.

I don't give much thought as to whether that's a good or bad thing because I've never *wanted* a thing or person so much, no matter how much time we have to spend apart or how much backlash comes as a result of it.

That's when it hits me.

Gabe King is my vice.

I just hope he's one of the good kinds—like chewing gum or sleeping in—and not one of those ones that will leave me heartbroken, sick, or somehow the worse for wear.

Gabe slides his hands over the silk material of my dress, and all rational thought ceases to exist in my mind.

Who cares about logic and planning and protecting myself when I'm reveling in the divinity of squirming under his touch?

Slowly, he works the garment over my head completely, eyes bugging out at the realization that I'm not wearing anything underneath.

He's still fully dressed, and as much as I love the look of him in a tux, I quickly unclasp his cuff links, then claw at his clothing until we're both fully bare.

"Julianna," he breathes as his hands grip the fleshy part of my hips.

I move on top of him, locking my arms around his shoulders and nearly combusting from how ready he feels beneath me. I grind my center against his erection as he sucks on my neck, and holy shit, I'm almost *there* already.

It's almost unbelievable how much pleasure I get from the sounds he makes, especially when they correspond with the tensing of his muscles and urgency of his lips against mine.

When he tugs at my nipples, I swear I see stars behind my eyes, but it's not until his thumb pads my clit while his middle finger curls inside me that I lose complete control. My orgasm floods all my senses, sending waves of pleasure all over my body.

It's so fucking good to be breathless and off-kilter, but as satisfying as that was, I want more.

Need more.

"I'll give you more," he growls.

I didn't mean to say that out loud, but I'm practically incoherent at this point, drunk off pleasure and him.

Gabe slides a finger inside me, and my hips buck against his palm as it nudges my oversensitive clit.

"I need you," I tell him, rocking back and forth.

"You have me," Gabe says, sliding another two fingers inside me, which causes me to cry out in satisfaction and a tiny amount of delicious pain.

I don't think I've ever felt this powerful or charged, like I'm going on simply what I want to do instead of what I should be doing—but in this case, they're one and the same.

Gabe King sits on an untouchable throne, according to millions of women around the world, but tonight, he's mine to explore and enjoy.

I slide off the couch, literally going weak in the knees, and drop down in front of him.

My mouth waters as I grip his cock, squeezing the velvety soft skin of his shaft.

I lock eyes with him as I drop my mouth to taste him, lapping up the trail of clear fluid from the tip and taking immense satisfaction in the number of curse words that he hisses through clenched teeth.

He locks his fingers in my hair as I take more of him in,

using my hands to pump what I can't fit in my mouth just yet.

"Julianna," he growls. "You can't keep this up. I'm too close."

I shake my head, sucking him harder with the intention of tasting him fully, but he pulls me off and shakes his head.

"You promised me shower sex," he says, his voice low. "I'm holding you to it."

He, apparently, means that in the literal sense because once we dash to the shower, the front of my body is against the tile as he thrusts into me wildly from behind.

The steam rises as we both find our release—me for the second time—then we both sink onto the shower floor, letting the water fall over us until we regain our bearings enough to towel off and collapse in bed.

Hours later, Pancake nudges me awake.

When she presses her wet nose against my skin, it's usually a welcome and endearing gesture, but I instantly find the exception in her touching my left butt cheek while I'm slightly hungover.

I shouldn't have nervously sipped that champagne—at least four glasses' worth—and the headache behind my eyes is a good reminder to never do that again. I stopped drinking early enough, but I was more focused on Gabe than on rehydrating later in the evening. I'm paying the price for it now.

But in all honesty, it's totally worth it.

Sighing happily, I stretch out in Gabe's ultra-comfortable bed.

I haphazardly shoved on one of his shirts before we fell

asleep, so now I'm cocooned in the scent of him, even if the man himself is nowhere to be found.

I sit up slowly, rubbing my eyes, and focus on the low tone of his voice.

The bedroom door is slightly ajar, enough for me to pick up the fact that he's on the phone and having a somewhat tense discussion.

My own phone tells me it's four o'clock in the morning, which seems ridiculously early for me, but that's when the bars close in New York. We barely made it to midnight last night. I can't imagine just getting home now.

I force myself not to eavesdrop on his conversation and focus all my attention on slowly downing the glass of water on his nightstand.

"That was Rina," he says grimly, running a hand through his very disheveled hair.

I'm momentarily stunned by his presence in the doorway and how perfectly sculpted he is, the lines of his body illuminated by the light of the hallway.

I can't believe I had sex with *that* last night.

Multiple times.

It's almost not fair that everything about him puts to shame every other experience I've ever had with a man.

I'm pretty sure I'm ruined for life.

"Is everything okay?" I ask, pushing that thought away as quickly as it came.

He sighs and rests a hand on the doorframe, not permitting himself entry to his own bedroom.

"Someone got a picture of us at the afterparty, then getting in the car alone together," he says reluctantly. "We should have probably left separately, or followed Zoe's instructions better, but I couldn't help myself."

"Oh," I breathe.

Being snapped out of my lust for Gabe is one thing, but being given news that's going to change my life is another, much worse feeling.

Once my identity is revealed to his followers, I'm going to be forever tied to him—not that our relationship is so serious just yet, but even if we don't work out, it's going to be something that potential employers, future boyfriends, or *anyone else* can find easily enough.

"Do they..." I stop myself and take a breath, trying to stay rational. "Is my name out there?"

He shakes his head. "But I think it's only a matter of time."

I see every emotion cross his face—desperation, unhappiness, guilt, shame for not protecting me from the inevitable.

As much as I love that he has let me in enough to see the realness about him, I don't like seeing these particular expressions on him.

"Come here," I order him, lifting the bedsheet.

He seems surprised at my gesture, like I should be having a total meltdown instead of embracing him.

Gabe sinks into the mattress, then sighs and pulls me back against his chest, enveloping me completely.

Even with everything I'm up against, I somehow feel safe enough in his arms to exhale and relax into him, tangling our legs together as he spoons me.

"I wish that being with me wasn't so..."

He trails off, then adds, "Complicated," at the same time I say, "Wonderful."

"I knew what I was signing up for," I remind him. "I know that being with you isn't like being with anyone else, but I don't know if you've noticed that I don't actually want to be with anyone else."

He presses a kiss to my neck.

"I don't want you to be with anyone else either," he says lightly. "Because I love being with you."

It's way too early for us to start throwing that word around lightly, and I'm glad my back is to him so he can't see the surprise—and slight panic—on my face.

"Rina is going to push everything off for as long as she can," Gabe says, brushing right past his admission. "You not having a social media presence makes this a lot easier, and she's been working on scrubbing any other personal information hidden in public records regarding you and your family since we first got together."

"She's really on it."

"Yes, but it's just really bad timing."

I can agree with that.

He's flying out later today to Los Angeles for a few meetings, one of which involves picking the next scent in his cologne and perfume contract. There's also some very exclusive ceremony and party put on by an acting association, which he briefly mentioned in passing, but I didn't know until someone congratulated him last night that he actually won an award for it.

It took me pressing the issue for him to admit he's actually really excited and honored by the recognition, and

Melanie's going to introduce him and present the award to him.

I'm moderately jealous I can't go.

But he kindly offered to take Angela with him to the airport since they're both flying out of JFK, and she was delighted to accept, promising me that she'd "grill him" along the way.

"It's fine timing," I insist.

Gabe has enough things to worry about, and I want him to enjoy his time in L.A. without feeling guilty about the upcoming wave of whatever's going to hit online.

"It's not like you're going completely off the grid," I continue. "Smelling prototypes then getting recognized for the work you do certainly makes you no less available than you are when you're on set."

Gabe runs his fingers along my side. "And you definitely can't come with me?"

"I'm sure you'll be winning plenty of awards in the future, Gabe King," I say.

He smiles at that. "I feel like I should be consoling you this morning, but you're the one making *me* feel better about everything."

I roll over to face him, taking in the worry lines etched in his forehead.

"Isn't that what a relationship is supposed to be like?" I ask. "Working through problems together and helping each other?"

"This is the first good one I've been in, so I'm not entirely sure," Gabe admits before he drops a kiss on my lips. "But I'll take it."

Pancake climbs on the bed with us, startling us both.

"Ugh," Gabe says, pulling the sheet more tightly over us, protecting our skin from her mass of fur. "You know, she never jumped up on the furniture until Zoe watched her over the summer."

"Come on," I encourage Pancake. "There's room for all of us up here."

Gabe smiles, giving in, and the three of us snuggle up, falling in and out of sleep until my alarm goes off at a more normal hour and it's time to take Pancake outside.

NINETEEN

As I mill about the kitchen while trying not to burn the omelette I'm making, I feel a little too at home in a pair of Gabe's sweats.

Maybe it's because the Finches have the same kitchen setup—which makes me wonder if Will is keeping our cooking tradition alive without me or has settled for whatever his parents are having—or maybe it's because of all the little comments Gabe has been making, combined with the way I feel for him.

That eventually, this could be my reality—nights out, good sex, dog walks, late breakfasts, and everything else that goes along with building a life together.

Eventually, Gabe and I are joined by our very hungover sisters.

They're still in their outfits and now-smeared makeup from last night while they nurse glasses of water, and Zoe's so out of it that she doesn't bother scolding Pancake for swiping a strip of bacon from her plate.

The four of us curl up in Gabe's living room and watch food competition shows, which I find to be kind of numbing and overall pleasant to watch, until it's time for Gabe and Angela to get ready for the airport.

By the time the car is ready, the girls have sobered up enough to be sad about Angela's departure.

I should be annoyed by the realization that my sister seems more upset about abandoning Zoe than me, but I actually think it's cute they've formed a bond, like it's further cementation of the Kings' place in our lives.

Gabe and Angela promise to text me before they take off on their respective flights, and I do get a little teary at telling them both goodbye, then Zoe and I link arms as we watch the car pull away.

Once they've turned a corner, Zoe dashes toward the elevator, looking a little green, while I take my time heading back to the Finch apartment.

And to reality.

Both Gabe and my sister leaving causes a ripple of sadness inside me, but I'm able to contain my emotion until I stand in the shower, letting the hot water wash away the remainder of my headache.

I go through the motions of washing my hair, scrubbing my body, and eventually toweling off, but I feel a little empty.

I know that Zoe's only a few floors away if I want some company, but it's not the same as having my boyfriend or my own sister around—even if her being here has made my room look like a tornado has come through it.

For the remainder of my afternoon, I clean. I put all my makeup back in its place, hang up my clean clothes, strip my bed, and put on fresh sheets, thinking that even if my mental space is a little off, my physical one is pristine.

And don't forget to tell Mom and Dad about Gabe, Angela reminds me as her plane starts boarding. *They'll want to hear it from you directly.*

I groan and know that, once again, she is right.

I bite the bullet and call them as I'm folding the last load of clean laundry, finding that I need to keep my hands busy while I talk about this.

They're a little taken aback by the sudden news of a relationship, especially it's with someone even they recognize—which is more than I could say for myself, obviously.

Apparently, he did a six-episode guest spot on one of their favorite crime shows.

It's a little surreal that they knew of my boyfriend before I did, but at the very least, they liked his performance and character, so they already have a somewhat good opinion of him. I know they're going to love him once they meet him because he's too charming to leave a bad impression on anyone.

My mom—in a weirdly Angela fashion—asks me dozens of questions, and I try my best to answer every single one.

We wrap up the call with her attempting to guilt me into bringing him home for Christmas, but I can't agree to anything without speaking to him or the Finches first.

All in all, it's a pretty good conversation, and I feel slightly relieved that it's done with.

The people I love are in the loop and supportive, but I'm not exactly eager to see what the rest of the world has to say about my relationship...

The next morning, I'm startled while buttoning my jeans by a pounding on my bedroom door.

I went to bed at a good time last night and didn't get a chance to see the Finches when they returned home, so I fully expect it to be Will, asking for breakfast and Pancake updates, but it's Amanda.

And she does *not* look happy.

"Peter and I would like to speak to you in his office," she says coldly enough that I shiver.

It doesn't matter that I've spent years studying human history; I'd recognize the sign of what's about to happen even if I never went to college.

I can't pretend to not know what this is about because I woke up to a flurry of text messages from Gabe with the news that my name has officially been leaked, along with more photos of us as well as with Zoe and Angela.

He warned me to stay off social media and to avoid searching online for now and to lay as low as possible because the backlash is at an all-time high right now.

I'm more than happy to go along with that plan; however, my sister is not. Angela has taken it upon herself to send me photos, screenshots of funny comments, and all of her favorite articles from gossip sites.

One I haven't seen, talking about how I'm some sort of gold-digging nanny, is up on Peter's screen as I step into his office.

A pit forms in my stomach, but I keep my composure as I wait for one of them to speak first.

"Care to explain yourself?" Amanda asks.

She gestures to the computer like I've committed some egregious felony that wrongs her very existence.

"It's true," I tell her slowly, promising myself to be as open and honest as I can so, at the very least, they can't accuse me of deception. "I'm dating Gabe King."

"Well, I can see that," she huffs.

"I have been for..." I blink, calculating just how short of a time, really, we've been together. "A little while."

Rage rolls over both Amanda's and Peter's expressions, and I can't help but fidget under their scrutiny.

Once again, it's Amanda who speaks first.

"How dare you use us like this?" she snaps.

"What?" I balk, purely out of confusion. "*Use* you? How?"

I regret my tone as soon as the words come out, but I'm so baffled that I can't help it.

"We overlooked your lack of experience because we thought you would be a good fit, given your academic background and desire to do well at the job," Amanda seethes. "But to use your access to our home and our building so that you could work your way into some sort of celebrity relationship is unacceptable."

"But that's not what happened at all," I sputter.

She holds up her hand. "I don't even want to hear it. How can I believe a word you say to me? You've broken our trust, Julianna."

I open and close my mouth a few times, unsure how to even begin to address this ridiculous claim. "I don't—"

"You're done here," she says resolutely.

I swallow. "Done?"

"You have until the end of the week to pack up your things and get the hell out of our lives," Amanda says evenly.

I expected yelling, scolding, and manipulation on their part—as is the norm I've unfortunately grown accustomed to—but to *fire* me over who I'm dating? This is a low I wasn't anticipating them to hit.

I'm so stunned that I don't blink until Amanda storms out of the room, and then my gaze lands on Peter's twisted smile.

"I warned you," he singsongs, leaning back in his chair and putting his feet up on the desk.

I pull at the ends of my hair and try to take deep, calming breaths, not trusting myself to speak.

Peter doesn't seem to notice the level of self-control I'm exhibiting because he just keeps pushing me further.

"Your relationship is completely inappropriate, and now you're facing the consequences."

I should be angry with Peter and Amanda for this situation, but really, it's my fault.

From the very beginning, I've had a firm idea of the type of people they are, and I let myself get complacent in my job and wrapped up in my life with Gabe when I should have been busting my ass with job applications and asking for introductions to Josh's network.

What the hell am I going to do now?

"Unless…I'm sure there's *something* you can do to make me convince my wife to call the whole thing off?" Peter says, eyes roaming over my body.

His implication catches my attention, and the way he's looking at me makes me want to crawl out of my own skin.

He stands up and doesn't stop moving until we're less than a foot apart, then reaches out and drags his hand up and down my arm.

I've been embarrassingly numb and shocked since I stepped into this office, but his insinuation and the feel of his skin on mine jolts me back to life, igniting a fire in me that burns too wildly to be put out.

My mind flashes with all the moments he has made me uncomfortable, all the lingering touches and glances my way, and the regret I feel over letting him see me in a tank top and shorts, and I get even more riled up.

"Peter..." I clear my throat so I don't mince my words. "You can go fuck yourself."

It's his turn to be baffled into silence.

I don't wait for his reaction.

I storm back to my room, yank out the two suitcases stored under my bed, and begin stuffing all my belongings into them.

In June, when I was packing to move up here, I had grandiose dreams of what my life would be like as I painstakingly and delicately packed everything I owned.

Now, I barely have patience to zip them shut before I leave my bedroom, slamming the door behind me.

I beeline for the front door, ignoring the fight between Peter and Amanda ensuing in the kitchen, but as I grab the knob, I catch Will's sad expression.

He hovers in the hallway, unsure of the reality he just walked into, and it shatters my heart.

"I'm so sorry, Will," I tell him.

I wish I could say more, explain what is going on and apologize for leaving him in such a crappy situation, but my tears fill my eyes.

The best thing I can do for him is leave before causing any further heartache.

Zoe doesn't question me when I show up at her front door with my suitcases and a line of frustrated tears down my face. She just lets me in and pulls me into a very firm hug until I've composed myself, then has me dump my bags in Gabe's room and curl up with her on the couch.

At some point, a mug of tea is forced into my hands, but it isn't until Gabe texts me a little later that I finally regain my voice.

"Please don't tell him I'm here," I beg Zoe, snapping out of my zombie-like state. "I know it's a lot to ask, to let me stay here and not tell your own brother, but I don't want to ruin his trip."

"You won't ruin his trip," Zoe assures me. "But I get it."

I swallow. "It's just—I know this means a lot to him, even if he's acting like it's not a big deal. He needs to enjoy this success and not worry about how I'm a little overwhelmed...and very unemployed."

She laughs at that, and eventually, I join her.

The rumbles of laughter roll over us, gaining momentum until we're at the point we can't say anything because we keep laughing, and I don't even remember what we originally found so funny.

We both wipe the tears from our eyes, residual giggles bubbling up every few minutes.

"How about I order pizza?" Zoe suggests.

"Pizza always sounds good."

"Tonight, let's just relax and stuff our faces, and tomorrow, we can figure everything else out."

I nod, filled with resolve. "Tomorrow."

TWENTY

While Gabe's away, he gives me the full Angela treatment, sending me pictures every few hours of what he's up to. I love to imagine myself in each setting right beside him.

I've never been farther west than Chicago, but I hope one day to go to the beaches, restaurants, and areas he visits.

For now, I buddy up with Zoe.

She seems thrilled to have a presence at home who isn't her brother or Pancake, content to sit with me while I scour the internet for any semblance of a job I'd be qualified for and an apartment to sublease.

I don't have luck on either front, and worse, every single time we leave our building, we get the attention of the dozen photographers who are staked out in front of it.

I make the mistake of wearing my infamous red scarf when Zoe and I head out to the grocery store and have to endure the taunts and questions screamed at me by the people behind their giant lenses.

After that, Zoe gives me a crash course in dealing with them—or rather, she encourages me to not engage with them in any fashion, even if they're complimenting me.

"If you even say as much as hello to one, they think they have an 'in,' and I swear they'll use it to make your life even worse."

"How?" I ask her.

"You'd be surprised how things can go from 'How's your day going?' to 'You're fucking your co-star, aren't you?' real quick," she says, then frowns. "At least, that's what Melanie says."

And so Zoe and I resolve to stay inside, ordering food and conducting apartment tours over FaceTime.

Unfortunately, one of the few promising leads, turns out, comes along with a roommate, who immediately recognizes my face when it pops up, then I'm subjected to a twenty-minute talk about how much she loves *Eggy Smith*—and if I'm moving in, would Gabe be around, too?

After what feels like the fiftieth failed attempt to find employment or housing, Zoe and I decide to have a mini-photoshoot in the living room for her social media feeds.

It starts off as a normal enough process, with her modeling clothes.

"I actually just got a box of new clothes from some online brand," she says. "Tell me what you think."

She saunters out from her bedroom, dressed head to toe in denim. "I guess they're trying to bring the Canadian tuxedo back in style? If it ever really was…"

"It's rumored that Bing Crosby actually is partially responsible for that phrase," I babble.

"The guy from that black and white Christmas movie my mom always loved?"

"I don't know which one that was, but probably. You see, he allegedly loved wearing denim so much that—"

"Wait," Zoe says, eyes flashing in excitement. "This could be a really cool series. I'll pick the looks, and you write the captions with your weird history knowledge. We could call it..."

I mull it over. "Factual Fashion? Couture Chronicles? Zoe Gives Me A Purpose Because I Don't Have One Right Now?"

She chuckles. "Whatever it is, I'm in on it."

Zoe plays dress-up while I capture her best angles, then fire off—with her approval—pictures to her feed.

It takes only a few hours for blogging sites and other influencers to pick it up, and we're both flabbergasted when her biggest account crosses the one million follower threshold.

She insists on celebrating, and although I'm not ready to drink champagne again, she has a massive box of macarons couriered over to our place.

We split each one in half, wanting to try every single flavor, and soon enough, we're on the couch in a sugar coma.

"I'm really glad you're dating my brother," she says to me, kicking off her heels.

"He's just a bonus to our friendship," I tell her. "But I do kind of owe you for orchestrating this whole thing."

She smiles. "You can thank me for all of this help by landing a kickass job and getting me one in a marketing department somewhere."

"No promises," I say with a laugh. "But I'll do what I can."

I think Zoe is so enthusiastic to help me get my act together partially because she still feels a little lost in her own life, but I enable it for the time being. I'm certainly not in a position to call anyone out on the state of *their* career or dole out any advice.

One of Zoe's friends—with benefits, according to her—hits her up to go out for a drink, and although she offers to stay in with me for moral support, I tell her to go.

I plan my own escape from the apartment, tucking my hair up into one of Gabe's beanies and begging the concierge to let me slip out the employee-only entrance.

With the first outside moment of anonymity in days, I walk over to the park and find the bench that Gabe and I once shared is unoccupied.

It's a cold December night, but I feel warm, wrapped up in my winter jacket and Angela's red scarf while I stare out at the water in darkness. The sight is peaceful enough to try to calm my chaotic mind.

And it helps that I spend at least fifteen minutes gawking at a picture of Gabe in another tuxedo that he sent, attempting to permanently embed the image into my brain.

Everything else seems so uncertain at the moment, but the way I feel for him...that's tangible, and I'm happy to cling to it.

My phone buzzes, and I can't help but smile when I see his name.

I miss you.

I swear, every single time I talk to Gabe, whether it's in

person or over the phone, those words are exchanged between the two of us.

If we end up working out and staying together for the long-term, I think that's going to be a regular phrase, based on his work schedule and...whatever I end up doing with my life.

But I have to accept that it's part of the deal when trying to be with someone in his line of work.

The public scrutiny hasn't fazed me too much to be more than a silly little annoyance, mostly because I haven't been thrust into the thick of it yet. Gabe and Rina have been shielding me from the worst of it, but I fear it will eventually wear me down.

Wanting to get an idea of the reality I'm facing, I decide to buck up and search my name.

Regret comes swiftly.

There are thousands of articles questioning my integrity and speculating on our relationship.

And somehow, the press got hold of one of my grade school yearbook photos and a few pictures of me from college, most of which are unflattering.

Whatever is on the internet is permanent, I know this from my own research, and these aren't exactly the images I would have chosen to showcase my life. I think of all the applications I just sent and how one search of my background will pull up all of these news articles, showing the slight controversy that could be attached to hiring me, and realize they're not even going to bother giving me a chance.

Worse, there's been an increase of scrutiny on Melanie because she and Gabe were photographed together yesterday outside her house in L.A., fueling even more speculation about me being a homewrecker.

I'm actually kind of impressed at the level of detail and collection of photos that gossip sites use to manipulate the story they want to tell, but eventually, it gets to be too much.

I shove my phone back into my pocket as the mental walls close in on me. I try to enjoy the night and the view, but it's shattered, so I walk back to the apartment, even though Zoe is out on a date and I'll still have to sit in silence there.

Angela calls me as I cross the street to the building, and I answer it enthusiastically.

"Hey!"

"Hey," she says back, voice breaking in the short syllable.

I stop moving. "What's wrong?"

Through her sobs, she tells me that Dad collapsed. It's mostly incoherent rambling about an ambulance ride, but there are two words that jump out at me.

Heart attack.

I made her a promise that I wouldn't act brashly if she told me the truth about what was happening at home, but this is not one of those instances when I should stay away.

The thought of my father lying in a hospital bed, hooked up to monitors, nearly breaks me in half.

"I'll be on the next flight out," I tell her. "Text me the details of where you guys are, and I'll be there as soon as I can."

Camera flashes blind me as I run toward the main entrance, and by the time I'm in the lobby, the spots of lights in my vision have barely subsided enough for me to pull up the airline app on my phone.

Booking this trip is going to put a big dent in my credit card, which I've finally wrangled under control, but I don't even second-guess myself as I purchase a ticket.

I'll have just enough time to grab my bags—which are still mostly packed—hail a cab, and make it to the airport shortly before boarding.

I press the elevator call button repeatedly, even though I know it won't have any impact. I learned all about the mechanics after my interest was piqued by a documentary on the history of elevators I caught on *National Geographic*.

"Come on, come on," I plead aloud.

Finally, the doors open, but before I can rush in, the Finches step out.

Because of course they do.

That's *just* what I need to deal with right now.

"What are you doing here?" Amanda shrieks.

"I don't have time for this," I tell them, pushing my way past them.

Amanda huffs. "I'll call security."

I surprise myself by snorting at her remark because I have Zoe's spare key, and by the time someone comes for me, I'll likely be gone anyway.

I press the correct floor and the door starts to close, but just as it's about to shut, Peter sticks his hand in, forcing it back open.

"Let it go," I snap, pressing the door close button.

Now that he's standing in the entrance of the elevator, it won't slide shut.

"Get away from our building and out of our lives," Peter says sharply.

I lose my cool.

"Is that really what you want, Peter? Because the other day, you implied that you wanted me to *prove* to you that I wanted to stay. Do you a big *favor* and all..."

I don't spell it out for Amanda because Will is standing there, confused and scared.

But by the way her face has gone from angry at me to furious at him, I'm guessing she picks up on my inference.

"And you're no better," I say to her. "Always putting me down and manipulating me into working overtime without pay because you know I don't have any options. God, it's a wonder you manage to keep anyone employed for longer than three months at a time. Oh wait, you *can't*. That's exactly what the agency said, that you 'drive them away.'"

I turn to face Will. "I'm sorry that you've been dealt a crappy hand with these parents, but know that you're a great kid. Truly, you're the best, and I'm so glad we got to know each other."

He offers me a small smile and a nod, and then finally, the doors close.

"Shit," I mutter to myself, wishing that confrontation felt as good as I imagined it would.

TWENTY-ONE

I hate the hospital—the smell, the sounds, the regular check-ins, and most of all, the fact that my father, lying in bed, looks as frail as I've ever seen him.

Whenever I talk to him on the phone, I imagine I'm talking to the version of him from when I was a teenager, when his hair was still mostly brown, when he'd have a joke for every scenario, and when he'd sweet talk my mom into baking nearly every single weekend—that's not the version of him I'm confronted with when I finally reunite with my parents.

They've both been endlessly supportive of my dreams. Even though I've racked up a tremendous amount of debt and found myself mostly unemployable, they've been there for me no matter how stressed out I was in grad school or how devastated they were when I told them I wanted to move away.

So it shouldn't surprise them as much as it does that

I've returned the favor and hopped on a plane at a moment's notice like they'd do if I were in trouble.

But this hospital room is small and suffocating, and all of us would much prefer to be at home on our cushy couch or sitting around our well-worn kitchen table.

On top of that, my dad has a surly roommate who sleeps most of the day, so we're all stuck whispering to one another in fear of facing his annoyed wrath.

We tried to bribe anyone who would listen to give us a better, single room—until we were informed that the insurance cost would double, then we decided we can make do as long as my dad is comfortable and gets the attention he needs post-angioplasty.

I'm lucky I missed the big, scary rush to the hospital and the waiting period as he went into surgery, and thankfully, the doctor says he'll be ready to be discharged within the next day or so.

Still, my mom, Angela, and I are a bit shaken from the entire ordeal.

My dad, however, is enjoying the attention immensely.

"All it took was a little heart attack to bring all my girls back together," he says as my mom fluffs the pillow behind his head.

"A little heart attack," I repeat incredulously.

My mom shushes me and tilts her head toward my dad's ornery roommate, whose snoring has petered off slightly.

I sigh and sit on one of the stiff chairs next to my sister, letting my tiredness set in. I came straight here from the airport, and we've all slept off and on while taking turns monitoring my dad.

Frankly, I'm surprised no one has kicked us out yet, but I think the staff is taking pity on us.

Angela shares her watered-down cup of coffee with me and offers me a very small smile. It's strange that I went six months without seeing her, and now we're together twice in one week—in two different states and under wildly different circumstances.

Scary medical things aside, my dad is right—it feels good that the four of us are back together.

I prop my feet up on my suitcase, the reminder that I'm essentially homeless for the time being.

I live in this hospital room now with all of my belongings. There's no place in New York for me to go back to, and I haven't told my family the news of my firing. It seems selfish to do so, all things considered.

My parents would welcome me home to my childhood bedroom, but that sounds almost as bad as living with the Finches.

And I certainly can't just move in with my boyfriend of a few months—that would be absolutely insane.

For now, I'll have to keep submitting applications, check my pride, and move back in with my parents until I have solid income and a place to live—maybe I can use Angela's name to mask my identity and find a sublease that doesn't require a security deposit or proof of income...

I shake off that impossibility because I'm being incredibly selfish and self-absorbed.

I don't need to concern myself with my champagne problems when my dad just had invasive surgery.

My focus needs to be here, right now, with my family—not the life I want that seems just out of reach.

"Who are you texting?" I ask Angela, noting her unusual silence.

We have severe boundary issues and not many, if any, secrets between us, so it's odd that she tilts her phone in a way that prevents me from seeing the screen, which tells me it's an intentional movement to keep something from me.

She ignores my question outright.

"Angela," I hiss in her ear. "Who are you texting?"

"No one," she says, shoving me away with her elbow.

"Then let me see it."

She holds the phone to her chest. "No! Mind your own business."

I jolt back in surprise, and I can see that she regrets her harshness.

"I'm sorry, it's just...don't be mad, okay?"

She turns the phone over to reveal Gabe's name.

"Zoe said you didn't want him to know, but I was freaking out about everything, and he's so calm under pressure, and I knew he'd be a good person to talk to—"

"How did you even get his number?" I ask slowly.

A devilish smile crosses her face. "We had a nice chat on the way to the airport."

"What does that mean exactly?"

"You know...doing my duty of grilling a potential suitor for my sister. I had to know if his intentions were honorable, blah, blah, blah."

I glare at her. "Angela."

"I had to know where he stood with everything," she says, defending her actions. "I mean, come on, Julianna.

He's him, and you're *you*. I wanted to understand how he felt."

My irritation is dampened by my curiosity. "And? What did he say?"

She smiles. "Enough that I knew he would want to know what was happening with Dad, even if it meant he had to take a red-eye to get here after accepting his award."

"What?" I nearly screech.

My dad's roommate sits up abruptly. "Keep it down!"

"Sorry," I tell him with a grimace.

He offers me a murderous expression before turning on his side and putting a pillow over his ears.

"He's on his way here right now," Angela says with a yawn. "He just texted me to say he grabbed a rental car at the airport."

"Shit," I mutter, then rifle through my suitcases for my toothbrush.

"You look beautiful," she says.

"Oh, shut up."

She laughs. "It's true, though."

"What's going on?" my mom asks us, picking up on the tension and my frantic movements.

"Gabe is on his way," I say.

"What?" She manages to keep her voice quiet, but her panic is evident.

"Blame Angela for this," I tell her, placing all the responsibility on my well-meaning sister.

My mom grabs the brush sticking out of my suitcase and runs it through her hair. "I don't even have my lipstick on."

"He's not going to care about your lipstick, Mom," Angela huffs.

"I care," she retorts. "Bill, can you...oh, nevermind."

My dad's in one of those standard-issue hospital gowns, giving the staff easy access to check him over, but I'm sure my mom wishes he was in something more presentable.

"Angela, clean up this mess."

My mom gestures to all the wrappers we've accumulated from the vending machine, then she tries to smooth my dad's hair and readjust his blankets to cover more of him.

I give my sister a smug expression before I head off to clean myself up in the bathroom.

"He's parking the car," Angela calls by the time I feel at least somewhat more presentable.

It's almost comical how the four of us sit trying to act normal when we're all a little on edge. My dad watches the television on mute overhead while my mom sits with ridiculously straight posture, and Angela crackles a piece of gum in my ear.

We sit in complete silence, making it easy enough to pick up on the slight commotion in the hallway that signals his arrival.

Gabe steps into the room, politely shrugging off the hospital staff.

"Thank you for the personal escort," he says, trying nicely to dismiss his followers. "I think I can take it from here."

Angela jumps up and shuts the door, having no qualms about being perceived as rude, and Gabe gives her a grateful nod before he turns, giving my parents his full attention and a big, easy smile.

He's still wearing his tuxedo from last night, but he removed the jacket, vest, and bowtie somewhere between Los Angeles and here, like he made a mad dash and left pieces of himself in the wake of his escape.

"Mr. and Mrs. Jones, it's so nice to meet you both," he says, setting down the tray of coffees and offering a bag of delicious smelling food to my mother.

My throat grows thick at his thoughtfulness.

"Oh, Gabe, how wonderful," my mother says, accepting his gesture. "This is so kind of you."

My father clears his throat and holds out a hand. "I would get up, but..."

"Of course, please don't," Gabe says quickly, returning the handshake. "How are you feeling?"

I'm frozen, watching my boyfriend interact so easily with my parents, smoothly carrying on a conversation on my dad's health and his own flight here.

"Why are you just standing here?" Angela asks quietly, nudging me with her elbow.

I snap out of my stupor and slide up to him, wrapping my arm around his waist.

He drops his arm around my shoulders, pulling me in for a half-hug while he continues telling my mom about the guy next to him on the flight who kept falling asleep on his shoulder.

My mom snorts as Gabe tells her that he eventually just relented and let the guy snuggle up against him, which brings another infuriated huff from the bed next to my dad's.

The man bolts upright once again and turns to us.

"How many times do I have to—" The words die on his lips when his gaze lands on Gabe.

Angela smirks at the guy's amazement.

He blinks rapidly. "Is that...are you...Gabe King?"

My boyfriend smiles at him, but I can see the trepidation in his eyes.

He definitely doesn't want to do this here—the attention from the staff before he entered the room appears to be more than enough for one day.

"I get that all the time," Gabe says dismissively.

Angela cackles and starts rifling through the bag of food with help from my mother, pulling out the vegetarian sandwich that Gabe apparently purchased with her in mind.

"Thank you so much for coming," I say quietly to Gabe.

"Of course." He kisses my temple. "I would rather have heard about what happened from you, though."

"I know. I just didn't want to ruin your night."

"Who cares about some award?" Gabe says.

"You do," I remind him.

"Not more than I care about you."

I squeeze his hand, finding that words fail me at the moment.

"I've told you before, Julianna, I'd rather be with you than anywhere else."

TWENTY-TWO

The capacity of the hospital room was limited even before I arrived, so with both Gabe and me now taking up space, my mom insists that we all head home to shower, sleep, and relax.

If it was just the four of us, I would have argued with her, but Gabe showing up changes things.

I know he didn't come here to be toured around or even treated as a typical guest, but I also can't expect him to sit around a cramped hospital room while my dad watches poker matches on television and ignores his surly roommate.

Gabe squeezes my hand as he drives me and Angela to our parents' house in his rented Honda Civic—a drastic change from his Lamborghini.

"I've cleared my schedule for the next week," he tells me.

"I know," Angela says from the backseat.

"What do you mean you know?" I ask her.

She laughs and continues scrolling on her phone. "All the gossip sites are talking about it. *Apparently,* you fled from a movie set because of some drama with Jules and Melanie and your 'torrid love affair.'"

"That's not even remotely accurate," I groan.

"They're making all sorts of royal puns...a few of them are actually kind of clever," Angela admits.

Gabe shrugs it off. "Rina will handle it."

"But isn't the studio going to be mad when you don't show up to work?" I ask him.

Gabe scoffs. "I'm not concerned about a massive studio losing a tiny fraction of their budget. I'm worried about my girlfriend and her father, who just had a heart attack and surgery."

"What about me?" Angela jumps in.

Gabe laughs. "I'm worried about you, too. And so is Zoe. She wanted to fly out, but I told her it wasn't necessary."

"Someone has to stay with Pancake," I say.

We finally pull up to our blue, two-story house, and I breathe a sigh of relief that it does, in fact, still feel like home. Then again, living with the Finches always seemed temporary, even if I did allow myself to get comfortable in their place.

Gabe and I carry our suitcases in with no help from Angela—who says she is going to go pass out on her favorite couch in the basement. His, of course, is a sleek matching set with designer logos, while I have two mismatched ones that definitely sat in our attic for ten years before I reclaimed them.

I watch Gabe take in my bedroom, its walls still the

same bright yellow I begged my mom to paint them back in high school, which are covered with posters of New York, along with a few pictures of Angela and me and some random friends I made over the years.

Everything is framed by the Christmas lights I strung up years ago, and although they're a little tacky, I plug them in and am happy when they still work.

"I like this," Gabe says, gesturing around my space.

It's definitely more *me* than the room I had in New York, but it feels like it belongs to a version of myself I no longer wholly relate to.

I went to Manhattan chasing a dream but without an exact plan for success, and without one, I failed.

Kind of spectacularly.

Now, I'm back where I started, but I'm definitely not the same person I was before I left.

In some ways, it feels like I've been beat up—by the Finches, the job market, the culture of the city, but I've come out stronger.

I don't have a clue what I'm going to do.

While I am a little embarrassed by my situation, somehow, I'm not stressing out about it. Maybe it's the fact that I've spent the last few days in a cloud bubble of nothingness with Zoe or perhaps it's because my father's heart put things into perspective for me, but somehow, I know it's all going to be just fine.

And part of that is because I am hopeful that Gabe will be by my side for all of it.

"I still can't believe you're here," I tell him as I kick off my shoes, flinging them into the bottom of the closet, just like I used to when I was a teenager.

Gabe glances at the stack of books on the shelf, mostly memoirs and travel books that I haven't looked at in years, but there is one well-loved steamy romance novel that sticks out from the rest—and, of course, it's the one he stares at the longest.

"I'm just glad your dad's going to be okay," he says, turning back to me.

"Me too. But you really didn't have to take off an entire week to be here."

"Do you not want me to be here?"

"No, that's not it," I say quickly. "I just mean you didn't have to do that for me."

"I wanted to."

He crosses the room and wraps his arms around my waist, and I don't immediately fall into him.

"What's this really about?" Gabe asks me. "Are you second-guessing things between us? Having doubts?"

I chew on my bottom lip. "I got fired."

He jerks back in surprise. "Are you serious?"

"Uh huh."

"All because you needed to be home for your dad?"

"No, it's because of who I am dating," I explain.

He sighs and runs a hand through his hair, looking even guiltier now than he did when the news of our relationship broke.

"They seem to be under the impression that I took the job for nefarious reasons, saying they can't trust me any longer," I say, finding humor in it. "I think they actually believe all of the headlines."

Gabe grinds his teeth together.

"It's fine," I tell him honestly. "It's...kind of a wake-up call."

"More like a wrongful termination lawsuit," he mutters.

I shake my head. "It's not worth all of that. Honestly, I'm just...I should have done this a long time ago. Not get fired but take more initiative into figuring out what I can do with my life aside from nannying for the Finches and serving as a walking encyclopedia. I'm going to keep applying to every job, fellowship, and internship I can find that even mildly interests me."

"You know, if it helps, I can make some calls—"

"No," I say forcefully. "You already passed my information along to Josh, which I more than appreciated, and now it's time I figured this out on my own. I need to do this, Gabe."

He nods in understanding. "So, when did this happen?"

"What?" I say, partially trying to deflect the question because I know he's not going to be thrilled with the answer.

He levels with me. "When did you get fired?"

"Um, a few days ago," I admit sheepishly.

"And you're just telling me now?"

I nod, not feeling great about it.

"Julianna," he moans.

"Sorry," I say with a grimace.

"No more secrets, please."

"Well, then, I should probably tell you that I've been living at your place for the last few days. I didn't have anywhere else to go, and since you weren't there—"

He chuckles. "Even if I was there, it's fine."

I take a small step away from him, needing him to see

me for who I am while I say the next few words. "I'm a homeless, unemployed girl from Ohio, Gabe. And you're...you."

"Come on," he says with a note of irritation. "I thought you were above all that stuff."

"I just don't want to drag you down into this pathetic spiral with me. I mean, hell, you just won your first big acting award, and instead of praising you for it, all anyone can talk about is some made-up love triangle."

"I thought being in a relationship meant we were going to be here for each other and support each other," Gabe says gently. "Weren't you the one who said that?"

I sigh and relent with a nod, letting him rub his hands along my arms.

"This isn't a big deal," he promises. "I've been raked over the coals by the press so many times, it doesn't even matter. Next time you and I step out in public, all of this will be forgotten, and they'll have found something new to talk about."

"Oh god," I say at the thought of repeating that ordeal. "Good thing Columbus isn't exactly a hotbed for paparazzi."

"Well, there were a few at the airport..."

I can't hide my surprise.

"It's fine, Julianna," Gabe says. "Just trust me."

"Okay," I say, putting everything I have into his judgment.

He nods once again. "Okay."

I step toward the bathroom that connects Angela's and my rooms, grateful that she had the foresight to pass out in the basement instead of her adjoining bedroom to give us some privacy. "I'm going to take a shower."

"Okay," he says, shifting on his feet.

"Are you going to join me?" I ask over my shoulder with a smile.

He follows me obediently.

Both of us together can barely fit in the shower stall, but we make it work, even though it makes me miss his oversized bathroom in New York.

In the days that follow, we sneak off when we can to go grocery shopping together or get some fresh air on a walk. I lead him on a tour around OSU's campus, then we get takeout for my entire family from my favorite Lebanese spot.

It feels normal for us to be together like this, but there's a level of excitement to even the most mundane tasks with Gabe. I am grateful for this little slice of time we get to spend with each other, even though we don't get a lot of it alone.

"I'm having fun with you," I tell him on the drive back from the drugstore where we collected a refill of one of my dad's prescriptions.

He reaches over and rests his hand on my thigh. "All of this time with your family has got me thinking about my own...specifically about what my mom told me before she died."

"'This is your life,'" I recall.

He nods. "I think people like going to movies because it gives them an escape from reality—I know that, and it's part of why I love being an actor. It's fun and challenging to feel different emotions and totally lose myself in something else. But we don't live in a reality where car chases happen and there's some sort of crazy, epic, dramatic storyline. It's just about living day by day with the people you care about."

I smile. "I agree."

"And that's what I think my mom was trying to tell me," he continues. "Yes, I am supposed to be aware of everything that's going on around me and appreciate what I have, but what's most important is the person you want to spend your time with...and for me, that's you. And I know it's sudden, but I already know that I love you, and I've just been trying to figure out a way to tell you."

The silence settles between us, and while I'm shocked by the timing of his declaration, I'm not floored by it.

In fact, it's almost a relief to know he feels the same way I do, and even though I've hoped for it, it's good to hear it out loud.

"You've been through a lot, I know," he attempts to say like he won't be gutted if I don't return those three words, "and you don't have to say it back—"

"I love you, too," I tell him.

In the movies, I believe there's usually a big kiss scene before the screen fades, but we're speeding along the flat road in his crappy rental car while a prescription bag and my purse sit on my knees, so we just exchange smiles every two seconds until we get back to my parents' house.

Before we head in through the front door, though, he tugs at my arm and pulls me in for a kiss that tastes like cinnamon.

EPILOGUE

FIVE YEARS LATER

"Are you ready to do this?" Gabe asks from the seat next to mine.

It's the question he always asks before we step out of the car and onto the red carpet. Usually, the events are for movies he or his friends are a part of, but for the first time ever, it's for us.

It's been five years since Gabe and I admitted that we loved each other, and although we said those three little words a little casually, it was a verbal agreement between the two of us that we were serious about starting a life together.

His first trip to Columbus wasn't under ideal circumstances, but it ended up giving us the time we needed to sit down and talk through our plans for the future, decide what we really wanted out of life, and determine our priorities.

And from there, we figured it all out together.

It helped that, halfway through our planning session

over Chinese takeout, I got a call from a consulting company that Josh recommended me to—they had a few projects that they desperately needed some research help on, and I was more than happy to lend my experience.

I always thought I would make it on my own and not leverage any connections I had, but they were so impressed with the work I had done for Josh that they were eager to speak to me.

That meeting led to more relationship-building and networking, and soon, I became overwhelmed with work, making a name for myself as the go-to researcher for several major studios.

Thankfully, I was able to do everything from my computer—although I did access local libraries when I had the chance—so I was able to witness more of Gabe's talent in person.

He's a truly phenomenal actor, but eventually, he confided that he felt a little handcuffed to his career. Making movies was fun for him, but he was interested in getting more ownership in the creative process, not just being a small piece of it.

After taking on a few producer roles and directing several episodes of television shows, Melanie actually suggested that with our combined brain power, we'd run one hell of a production company.

And that's how The Good Life Productions came about.

Starting the new venture wasn't without hiccups—we both came with passion but minimal experience, and together, we had to navigate the waters of fundraising, reading hundreds of scripts, and suffering many sleepless nights.

All of that has led us to this moment, to tonight, and the premiere of our first film.

The project is a small, ambitious, indie-feel movie written by an unknown writer—well, unknown until we came along—but Gabe and I were immediately drawn to the script as we combed through the endless stacks of potentials.

We threw ourselves completely into the process as Gabe finished out his contractual obligations with other studios. I followed him around the globe, working remotely and memorizing what I could about whatever rich culture was offered wherever he filmed.

On our second anniversary, he proposed while we were vacationing in Paris, and on our third, we got married in a small ceremony in Columbus, then quickly followed it with a honeymoon in the Bahamas, where Ruby and Melanie finally tied the knot with Gabe as the best man.

Melanie's coming out—and subsequent marriage announcement—made the biggest splash of headlines I'd seen yet, but it was also overwhelmingly positive.

Somehow, just like I once hoped so desperately, everything worked out just fine.

There's an impatient tap on the top of the car before Zoe wrenches the door open. "Come on, kids," she says. "I'm getting antsy."

"Is it an excited antsy or an I-need-a-cigarette antsy?" I ask her.

She groans. "You know not to say the c-word, sis. Now it's all I can think about."

Gabe laughs while Zoe starts shifting from side to side.

"Here," he says, offering up a piece of cinnamon gum. "This'll help."

"There's no nicotine in that, Gabriel," Zoe retorts, taking it anyway. "Come on. You can't be late to your own movie."

"Ready?" Gabe asks me again.

I nod, and he steps out of the car and offers me a hand, which I accept gratefully—I don't know how anyone gets out of low cars in high heels and designer dresses without help.

"Cute," Zoe hums, snapping a bunch of photos on her phone.

She's in charge of all social media and marketing for our production company, and she's been taking night classes to earn her MBA. Occasionally, she'll pull Angela in for some freelance design work, making it a truly family-run business.

I've loved seeing their friendship grow over the years and witnessing them have professional and personal success. They've been the biggest cheerleaders for everything Gabe and I have set out to do, and I'm lucky to have both of them in my life.

"Now go kill 'em," Zoe urges, patting us both on the back for good measure.

Then we're off, gliding down the red carpet and posing together.

It took me at least five of these events to feel somewhat comfortable with the process, and that *after* I took posing classes—yes, those exist—to help my nerves.

Gabe and I are in sync as we work the event, stopping

for interviews with some of the journalists and television personalities we've built relationships with over the years.

Josh, Melanie, and Ruby arrive, followed by my parents, Angela, and Gabe's dad, then we, along with Zoe, all pile in for a group photo. I know it won't be used in any publication, but it will be nice to have the memory just for us.

Once we finish up with the carpet and are ushered inside, we each collect our popcorn bag, fountain drink, and a little memento from the film—which Zoe insisted we have because it will encouraging people to post pictures and help build up buzz.

Gabe and I don't watch the film with everyone else in the theater.

Instead, we hang around backstage, watching the audience's reaction, and lightly chat with some of the crew members.

Two hours later, the end credits roll, and there's nothing but excited chatter and laughter in response to the movie, which makes us both grin widely.

"This is our life," I tell him, reaching for his hand.

Gabe smiles and drops a kiss on my lips. "Let's live it."

We step on the stage, together, to roaring applause.

ACKNOWLEDGMENTS

My husband once told me that any book I write in New York City, it's like adding a major character to my novel that doesn't have any dialogue—and it's true. I lived in Manhattan for eight years, and this book is somewhat of a love story to what I experienced while living there.

I'm also very lucky that my dearest friend Steph (who this book is dedicated to) got me "in" on a list to attend movie screenings and premieres, which really helped shape some of the more Hollywood-centric elements of this book. I'll never be able to repay her for getting me those experiences or for all of the love she has given to me over the course of our friendship, and I'm so grateful to have found her!

I have to give a big shoutout and virtual hug to Jen McDonnell who did some serious editing work on this manuscript and made me laugh out loud along the way.

Also, Lindsay Hallowell, thank you for saving me from

myself (and all my grammatical errors) so many times. I'm ridiculously grateful to have you as part of my team.

I'm so grateful to Denise, Emily, my network of beta readers, ARC reviewers, and book bloggers who advocate for my work so fiercely—your support means so much to me.

Finally, my family and close friends who keep me sane throughout the process, I can't thank you enough for letting me ramble on about what I'm working on and everything else you do.

ABOUT THE AUTHOR

Jennifer Ann Shore is the award-winning and bestselling author of several fiction books, including "Metallic Red," "The Stillness Before the Start," and "The Extended Summer of Anna and Jeremy."

In her decade of working in journalism, marketing, and book publishing, she has gained recognition for her work from companies such as Hearst and SIIA.

Be sure to visit her website (https://www.jenniferannshore.com) and follow her on Twitter (@JenniferAShore), Instagram (@shorely), or your preferred social media channel to stay in touch.

CPSIA information can be obtained
at www.ICGtesting.com
Printed in the USA
FSHW022219010821
83733FS